W9-ABN-280

HAVING BEEN THERE

Compiled and edited by
ALLAN LUKS

Introduction by
RING LARDNER, JR.

CHARLES SCRIBNER'S SONS
New York

1 3 5 7 9 11 13 15 17 19 O/C 20 18 16 14 12 10 8 6 4 2

Printed in the United States of America
Library of Congress Catalog Card Number 79-84843
ISBN 0-684-16170-2

ACKNOWLEDGMENTS

About two years ago I began talking to authors and alcoholism professionals about the idea for a collection of original, modern short stories portraying all phases of alcoholism's personal drama. They applauded this natural combination of literature and the struggle with alcoholism, since both concern man's attempts to understand himself and act on this awareness. But then I was left to experience the self-doubts and practical difficulties that time brings. The continued encouragement I received from Jerry Harmon —writer, advertising executive, and recovered alcoholic— kept me going.

When 513 short stories poured into my office from writers from all parts of the United States, I needed help to read the manuscripts properly. Mary K. Harmon, a veteran book editor (and Jerry's sister), stepped in to read these manuscripts and offer comments on them for my review.

After a group of finalists were selected, the stories needed to be judged by writers who "had been there." Ian McLellan Hunter, TV and movie scriptwriter, and Ring Lardner, Jr., novelist and screenwriter, generously volunteered their time in grading these manuscripts; although I, of course, was responsible for the stories finally chosen.

The board of directors and staff of the New York City Affiliate of the National Council on Alcoholism, especially Lois Jesberger, provided constant support; Harry Smith, poet and publisher, offered important suggestions; and Laurie Graham, my editor at Scribners, was unfailingly helpful in developing this collection.

—Allan Luks

CONTENTS

INTRODUCTION

I have lived, boy and man, among writers and drinkers for more than sixty years. The first two drunks in my life were Sinclair Lewis and F. Scott Fitzgerald. I never saw my father in a state I could then identify as intoxication, but that was because he maintained a sober bearing longer than most heavy drinkers, and was at his most circumspect in the presence of his sons. By the time I became fully aware of his illness, other ailments had put him on the wagon most of the time.

In the forty-five years since he died, during my adult life in New York and Hollywood, writers, especially drinking writers (we seek each other out), have always been in the majority among my friends. I have also accumulated a store of information from written and oral sources about other twentieth-century American writers, beginning with my father's generation and including the latest to make a mark in the profession. In these ways I have come to know that we have a special susceptibility to the drug which one of the addicts, Ernest Hemingway, described as the "Giant Killer." I don't agree with Gore Vidal, if he is correctly quoted, in the statement that "almost all male American writers are alcoholic." But I took strong exception when, in a recent questionnaire on the subject, men as diverse and distinguished as Alistair Cooke, Peter De Vries, Ira Levin and Michael Crichton all felt writers were no more likely alcoholic prospects than members of other professional groups.

My own conviction on the matter is supported by the fact that more than five hundred stories were submitted for this collection after it was announced in a number of periodicals aimed at writers. Further evidence in the same direction came from the stories themselves. They varied considerably in quality, but almost every one of them had a ring of authenticity that suggested the material came from the author's experience. Of course, empathy for the struggles alcoholism creates does not necessarily indicate firsthand experience with the illness. But in reading these stories I often felt that alcoholism had played a part in the authors' lives.

It isn't too hard to think of reasons why writers are more likely to succumb to alcoholism than most people. It is more feasible to alternate working and drinking periods when you fix your own hours, and much easier as a result for the addiction to settle in unrecognized. Writing is lonely work, and loneliness is one of the afflictions allayed by alcohol and other sedatives. Writers traditionally suffer an aching need for recognition and frequent traumatic failures of confidence in their ability to achieve it. Alcohol assuages all these pains with equal efficiency.

My father's alcoholism, however, developed at a time

when he was working regular hours, surrounded by people, and so devoid of ambition he hadn't even considered the idea of writing a piece of fiction. The pains of creation, the lonely struggle to conceive a short story already bought and paid for—that came later, and he consistently sought relief from the strains of work in a balancing period of involvement with the bottle. But by that time the cure was more debilitating than what it was supposed to mitigate.

You could say that makes Ring Lardner's case exceptional, but what's really more to the point is that every alcoholic is an exception. That's one of the aspects of the disease that has made it so hard for people to accept it as a disease. A straightforward ailment like beriberi or scarlet fever has a definite, traceable cause, a range of time that can elapse before the symptoms become manifest, and either a specific remedy that will produce a cure if applied soon enough, or an expected duration before it departs regardless of treatment. There is nothing that predictable about alcoholism (although it is our oldest recorded drug addiction) except a steady deterioration that can be checked short of death only by treating both the physiological and psychological dependence. There is no one type of person who becomes alcoholic, and the ways people behave in the throes of the illness are as varied as human personality.

The eighteen stories in this book reflect that variety of human drama in lives changed by alcohol addiction—lives not only of drinkers but of their spouses, children, friends, lovers and employers. They also reveal, in the structure of their presentation here, the overall sameness in the pattern of dependence, deterioration and, sometimes, recovery. Collectively, they reject the old moralistic judgment that the compulsive drinker suffers from a fatal character defect. They are based instead on the modern scientific finding that alcoholism is an illness and that it can be treated, even if we can't divide the blame precisely among biochemical, psychological and cultural causes.

Within the general theme and these basic truths, each story selected for inclusion here presents a different and provocative situation. A child plots to have his alcoholic father beaten. An exploited housewife treats herself to one beer per washing-machine load, and ends up on the laundry-room floor. Even a bartender's patience is tried as two contrasting regulars turn into grotesque caricatures of their sober selves. A recovered woman braves a cocktail party and watches the coffee cup shake in her hand. A physician diagnoses the irreversible damage to an alcoholic who has refused therapy. And a husband regards Alcoholics Anonymous as a rival during his wife's rehabilitation.

A work of art must do more than portray a situation or tell a story. Consider the first title in this book, Marjorie Lucier's "Vacancy." On the surface we are given a touching picture of self-sacrifice with a premonition of tragedy. But without imposing her editorial judgment, the author makes us ask questions that go beyond the range of the narrator's observations. Is the "sacrifice" itself contributing to the tragedy? What is the most loving response to a lover's course of self-destruction?

Insights like these into the phantasmagoric world of the alcoholic and the people around him or her are essential to our understanding of what it's like to have been there.

—Ring Lardner, Jr.

Their Children, Spouses, Lovers, Brothers...

VACANCY
by Marjorie Lucier

The faded blue-and-white sign swung stiffly in the ocean breeze. Hinged quarter boards made a series of descending announcements:

SAND DUNE MOTOR INN
TV in Every Room
Starfish Lounge
Pool
Vacancy

In the lobby I was greeted by a short, mournful man with carefully combed brown hair and huge brown eyes, which he rolled in the manner of a nervous horse. Behind him, at a desk littered with papers, sat a platinum Barbie doll (his wife, I later learned) in polka dot shorts and ruffled halter top. She flashed me a plastic smile.

"Do you still have that vacancy?" I inquired.

"Do I still have that vacancy?" he exploded. "Listen,

lady, you know how many vacancies I got? Forty-two, that's
how many. You know how many of these goddamned units I
got rented? Eight, that's how many. I'm going broke, for
Chris' sake. All those cars driving by—where they goin'
anyway, for Chris' sake! I put on all those extra units last
year, and this year nobody comes. You want a unit? Give you
the best one in the place. Overlooking the pool, but quiet, you
know?" He reached out to the board without looking, and
took down a key attached to a wooden disk and threw it on the
desk. "Don't ask me how much. Believe me, I'll make it real
cheap. I'm starving to death anyway."

Prying myself away from my bankrupt host, I drove over
to my unit. The room was decent but dull, in the manner of
good motel rooms everywhere. I tossed my luggage on the bed
and walked out to the pool.

Two small boys splashed at one end. Across the pool a
middle-aged couple sunned themselves on lounge chairs.
Near the entrance to the lobby, a blond young man was
drinking beer from green bottles and setting up the empties
in a long row. He winked at me in a friendly fashion and
belched gently.

I settled down to enjoy the sun and sea breeze, and
started to doze, when my host came out of the lobby. He
started fussing around the pool, straightening the chairs,
picking up old paper cups, and grumbling.

"Why don't you go down to the bar and have a drink?
Got the best bartender on the Cape down in the lounge. Much
good it does me. Costs me a fortune, just like everything else.
A fortune for insurance on this goddamned pool, just in case
some nut drowns himself." He glared at the little boys, who
splashed away, uncaring.

Apparently the only way I was going to escape my host
and his troubles was to follow his orders to go down and have

a drink, so I felt my way down the dim stairs to check out the bartender. The place was dark and air-conditioned to a chill. Behind the bar the wall was filled with an aquarium where small fish swam through plastic ferns and seashells from Woolworth's. The bar was presided over by Stevie the Greek, a tall, homely man, with hair combed forward to cover a bald spot, wearing faded jeans and a string of love beads. He was listening patiently to precise instructions on how to construct a dry manhattan from a serious young man who seemed to have great doubts that Stevie could manage the twist of lemon.

"What are we here, barbarians?" Stevie asked, wriggling his heavy eyebrows at me as he threw the cocktail together without looking and popped it in front of the customer. "Think that'll make it, boss?"

There were only a few of us at the bar, drawn into the kind of distant camaraderie you feel in such places. The fish swam lazily behind the lighted glass, the air conditioner whirred in the corner, the empty tables stretched away into the darkness. Glasses clinked. People talked about where they had eaten the night before. A man in a Budweiser hat kept saying, "You give me a good steak, and you can keep the rest of the crap." The bored-looking woman with him must have heard this many times before, because she shot him a look of pure hatred each time he said it.

Our lugubrious innkeeper came down to check out the receipts and groan. He cast his huge brown eyes up to the ceiling, where dwelt his private deity. "They're killing me, for Chris' sake."

We were joined by the Barbie doll, shivering in her halter top. Stevie turned on the television set to the baseball game, and everyone watched except me, so I was the first one to notice the new arrivals.

HAVING BEEN THERE

The woman came down first, holding tightly to the hand of the man behind her. Her face was interesting, but hardly beautiful. Eyelids too heavy, cheekbones too high, a mouth that drooped a little. Her one really beautiful feature was her hair. Thick and lustrous, it was pulled back from her face and piled on top of her head in a shining crown. The man was hawk-faced. A hungry, aging Viking, with longish blond hair turning white, dressed in an aloha shirt and tight Levi's.

The woman stopped at the bottom of the stairs and looked around carefully, her eyes quickly checking the little dance floor and the piano at one end. The couple drifted over to the bar and ordered beers. The man drank his, quickly, thirstily, but the woman left hers untouched. After a few minutes, she rose and strolled casually to the piano, and sat down. I watched her idly, wondering what she was doing. Everyone else was glued to the ball game. Except the Viking. He never once took his eyes off her.

She touched the keys lightly, and then broke into a light, popular song. Stevie leaned on the bar and listened, a few heads turned her way. At the end of the song, there was a spatter of applause. She smiled her thanks and swung into another number, a little louder now. The light at the keyboard illuminated her face from below, and I could see that she was not as young as I had thought at first. I was surprised, too, to note that she was wearing false eyelashes and very careful makeup. On a hot July afternoon on the Cape, this was most peculiar. Casual living was the keyword, and getting all dressed up meant putting on your shoes in most cases. She looked like somebody who was applying for a job.

The middle-aged couple I had seen at the pool came down, and the pianist started to play "Tie a Yellow Ribbon." They kicked off their sandals and broke into an old-fashioned jitterbug. Soon everyone at the bar was clapping hands and singing along. They cheered loudly at the end, and called for more. The woman at the piano swung into "Feelings" and started to sing. She had an astonishingly beautiful voice, trained and true. Everyone was turned to her now, the room was still. Our host tiptoed over to shut off the air conditioner. The song was perfect, and when it ended, everyone cheered.

Stevie went over to offer her a drink on the house, but she only smiled and shook her head. The Viking accepted, though, a double bourbon, which he tossed down along with her beer. She watched him for a moment with an odd expression, then started a slow introduction on the piano, and started to sing—can you believe it?—the *"Un bel dì"* aria from *Madama Butterfly*. Every note was like crystal. Even the man in the Budweiser cap and his bored wife shut up and stopped rattling their ice. She had them all hypnotized. But there was something funny about the whole thing. It didn't ring spontaneous and true. But I couldn't figure out what was wrong.

The blond marathon beer drinker stumbled down the steps and stayed. More people drifted in from outside. Our host was joyous. His brown eyes shone moist in the gloom.

"She's terrific, for Chris' sake!" he whispered hoarsely. "What a drawing card she would make—if I could just get her to stay. We would pack this place every night. I could even put an ad in the paper."

I could see him mulling over the cost. He leaned over the piano to pat her on the shoulder. She smiled at him, never stopping her hands on the keyboard. The Viking watched. He smoked constantly, long, thin, cork-tipped cigarettes right down to the tips. Stevie offered him another drink, and he gulped it down thirstily.

"Her name is Tina," my host announced, settling

himself beside me once more. "I told her I'd advertise her in the papers and everything. 'Tina Plays and Sings for You,' or something snappy like that. She ain't even staying anyplace yet. There's just the two of them, so if I gave her a unit, too, she might stay and work for me. What the hell, there ain't anybody staying in the units anyway. Betcha we could fill the place up every night." He waved his hands at the empty tables. "What do you think?"

"She'll stay all right," I told him. "That's what she came in here for."

"You're crazy. She's been really big time, can't you tell? Did you hear that voice? She don't have to work places like this. I'll be lucky if I can get her, for Chris' sake. Why should a dame like that need a job here? She's got real class."

I didn't know why, but everything she had done seemed to be a charade she had played out many times before. "I think she's auditioning for you right now," I told our host. "They're probably broke, her guy is awfully thirsty, and she's trying to get them in out of the storm."

"There ain't no storm out here." He looked puzzled. Encouraged by my remark, he approached her again.

"Whaddya say, Tina, old kid. Why don't you stay and work for me, huh? Come on upstairs and we'll talk business."

She raised her eyes again and looked at the Viking with the same odd expression, and then she smiled, a twisted halfhearted smile. They exchanged a long, deep look, so full of significance that the air seemed to tingle with it. His face crumbled with a look of terrible love and pain, and he sagged against the bar as if exhausted. We made it, baby, we made it, her eyes told him. Without a word, she rose and followed our host to the stairs. Then she turned and looked back at the Viking.

"Honey," she called. Her voice sounded so small when

[8]

she wasn't singing. "Honey—come with me?" She waited until he joined her, and holding tight to each other's hands again, they went up to the office.

In the days that followed, Tina was indeed a sensation. Word spread that the Starfish Lounge had that rare thing, a real talent. Pleasure-seekers came from all over the Cape to hear her. The cash register jingled, and our host even stopped complaining about his empty units. But Stevie was a little disgruntled because Tina seemed impervious to his charms.

"The only time I see her is when she's working, or she comes running down to get cigarettes for him. I tried to cozy up to her once, but she ran out of here as if he might drown himself if she wasn't there to save him." He polished a glass thoughtfully. "Funny dame. What do you suppose she sees in that bum? He's killing her, leeching off her like he does, and she's killing him, too, in a way. That's a funny thing for me to say, isn't it? After all, drinking is my business. Wonder why she does it. That guy is an albatross around her neck."

The Viking had become a real pain in the Starfish Lounge's paradise. Never far from Tina's side, he now had money to drink as he liked and it soon had become apparent that he was an ugly drinker. He always took the same seat at the end of the bar where he could watch her, and as the evenings wore on he became increasingly loud and troublesome. Even Stevie, used to good-natured handling of heavy drinkers, usually left him alone. Soon no one would sit next to him, even when there was standing room only.

Tina played on, and sang with seeming serenity, her voice never wavering, but her face had taken on a curiously blind, closed look. Sometimes the Viking, leaning forward to focus on her face, would fall onto the floor, swearing loudly, but she paid no attention. We were all embarrassed and apprehensive about what he might do next.

During her breaks Tina would go and stand beside him, putting her hand on his arm, so that for that short time at least, his busy glass was still. Once, when I was standing close by, I watched her bury her face in his shoulder, and the Viking put his arm around her and held her gently. They stood there together, alone in that noisy place. Stevie shot me a significant look and raised his eyebrows in wonderment.

After a while, even our host, who was hardly anxious to cut off the golden shower that was saving him from The Bank, asked her jokingly, "Hey, Tina, can't you talk to your guy? He's putting the squash on everything we're doin' here. Maybe I could give him his own bottle, and he could have his little nips back in your room where it's quiet, huh?"

"Oh no," said Tina, looking alarmed. "I need him here with me." So he stayed. He seemed to be accumulating booze after a long dry spell, and with it all the anger and resentment he could pack into his thin body intensified. It followed, of course, that before more than a few nights had passed, he had tried to pick a couple of fights with paying customers, and Stevie had to step in and threaten to shut him off if he didn't quiet down.

The weather remained glorious, and since I still had a week of vacation left I decided to stay on and enjoy it. Also, by now I was intrigued by the mystery of Tina and the Viking and wanted to see what was going to happen next to this pair of lost souls. The days I spent half dozing by the pool; and the evenings in the lounge, where things were now swinging to all hours, were pleasant. I learned that the blond beer drinker was, of all things, an accountant who lived with his married sister and always spent his annual vacation in just this way.

"I have to take three weeks and just get blotto," he told me. "Otherwise I couldn't make it through the rest of the year." He was, actually, a rather gentle, pleasant young man, and I asked him why if he found his life so intolerable he did not make some changes in it.

"Oh, you don't understand," he said broodingly. "Nobody understands."

End of *that* conversation, but we started to make little bets on how long it would take the Viking to get smashed and ugly each night. He was arriving at the bar earlier and already high. Tina looked a little tired, her mouth drooped a little more, but she was outwardly calm, carefully groomed. She sang on. Our bets were paid off with much giggling and sham secrecy. Then I stopped betting because I realized every time, win or lose, there was a dull feeling of shame connected with it, as if I had taken part in some small act of cruelty.

How can an outsider understand why two people need each other? Was she weak or was she strong—or was he the strong one that she needed in spite of his flaws? Well, I'd probably never know.

Finally, on Saturday night it happened. The place was mobbed, and the applause enthusiastic. It was only about ten o'clock when the sound of splintering glass stopped all the noise. The Viking was on his feet, weaving, swearing thickly, the blood running from his hand, which clutched a broken glass. He was trying to attack one of the men at the bar, but was staggering too badly even to get to him. Somewhere a woman screamed.

Tina left the piano in one quick, fluid movement. She took the glass from him and set it down. Then, her arm around his narrow waist, she slowly guided him around the bar and up the stairs. His blood dripped slowly and steadily onto the carpet. No one rose to help her. The room was filled with embarrassed silence.

"Come on, everybody, who needs a refill?" Stevie asked,

trying to get things back to normal. I could see our host in the background, his head in his hands.

I couldn't just sit there without knowing if everything was all right, so I went out to see, uneasy, not wanting to poke my nose into somebody else's business. Tina was making it across the parking lot, the Viking leaning heavily on her shoulder. Their dusty black sedan was parked in front of their room, and she opened the door on the passenger side and maneuvered him into the front seat. Then she went into their room, and soon came out carrying two suitcases, leaving the door open and the lights on behind her. She tossed the suitcases into the back seat and got behind the wheel. The engine started with a fearful clank and roar, and the car lurched forward. So did the Viking. He flopped against the dashboard and banged his head on the windshield. I saw her reach out her right arm and gently ease him back against the seat, as one would a child. He slumped down, his head against the side door.

I hurried to the car and called in the window. "Will you be all right?"

Tina stared ahead, that curiously blank look on her face again. There was no anger there or tears.

"He'll be all right," she said.

Not "We'll be," or "I'll be," but just "He'll be," as if I must naturally have been asking after him. I wasn't.

"I'll have to find another place now."

She sounded so lonely, so very lonely.

She drove slowly out of the lot and down the drive toward the roaring traffic, waiting patiently for a break in the line of cars rushing down Route 28. Then she pulled out. I ran to the entrance and watched the red taillights of her car join the hundreds of others as they disappeared over the hill into the darkness.

GOLD RINGS
by M. de Koning Hoag

My father was a big man, wide over the shoulders, with muscled arms and strong hands. Any dad is big when you're a kid and stand only up to his belt buckle. In time his bigness is not so much a physical thing as a feeling. When he can't carry you on his back anymore and he stops blowing on your neck because you're too old to be held and blown on, there are other things.

Like the day when he says, "Come on, Julius. Let's ride the horses!"

Dad would park the car on the Playland lot and we'd race together down the cement walk, through the turnstile, to the concession rides.

"The big thing," he would say, "is to get the gold ring."

"There isn't any ring," I always answered.

Then for the hundredth time he'd tell me about the gold ring. The music of the merry-go-round mingled with the roar of the roller coaster, the screaming of girls, and the crashing of bumper cars. The racket got my ears tingling. But it was always the merry-go-round we headed for—the white, brown, and black horses, plunging up and down in their calypsoed circle.

"When I was a kid riding the horses," Dad would go on, "once every round we reached up to grab the brass ring. You had to be at the top of a gallop. Sometimes the ring was a gold one and you got a free ride." He would laugh aloud, remembering, and I was proud that people around us laughed too.

My father always sat on a horse on the outside. As we whirled, he would reach high and far, making an imaginary swipe in the air, pretending to loop a ring on his finger. When the ride was over, I'd unbuckle my strap and jump down, shouting, "Did you get a gold one?" knowing that he'd say, "Sure thing!" Then he'd fish another ticket out of his pocket while I climbed back on my horse, waiting for the music to begin another crescendo.

Afterward, he'd buy me a cherry ice and get himself a beer, swallowing deeply.

There was a camping trip I remember, some years later, the spring before my twelfth birthday. Dale and Kevin and I were allowed to pitch our three pup tents a little way from those of our dads. When we finished singing and telling stories, exchanging usually forbidden words, laughing at the jokes our fathers told that we didn't always understand, we crawled into our sleeping bags, shutting ourselves into khaki and nylon.

I woke up after midnight, having to go to the bathroom. I wiggled out of my bag and peered out the tent flap.

Gold Rings

Everything was black with shadows and I had no flashlight.

Walking carefully over ground and rocks and loose branches, half fearful, half brave, I crossed to my father's tent. The Coleman lamp was still flaring. My father was sound asleep.

"Dad... Dad..." I whispered, but my voice didn't rouse him. I knew about leaving lanterns unguarded, so I shook him and finally roused him.

"I need a flashlight; it's dark out there."

"No darker going back than coming," he mumbled and flopped over with his eyes closed.

"How about the lantern being on?"

"Turn her off." His suggestion that I crawl in with him and be warm and not alone didn't come, and I was too old to ask. I reached over and turned the screw that shut off the light. Next to the lantern stood an uncorked brown quart bottle. I didn't think about that bottle then, and hardly remembered it afterward. Until years later.

We hiked the next day, making trails, playing ambushes, collecting rocks and leaves. That night Dad told his funniest stories. And that night he fell into the camp fire. Gesturing and prancing around, he stumbled. All of us shrieked as sparks flew up and the other dads pulled him free. His right sleeve was burned to shreds and the skin singed underneath. He laughed it off, proving that he was not only funny and wonderful, but brave.

The next day the arm swelled up, red-streaked and blistered. It was Sunday and we had to pack up and go home. I was kind of scared because of the arm, but the rest of the dads seemed to be more mad than sympathetic.

At home I had to do the unloading, shaking out the bags and hanging them out to air, cleaning up the cooking stuff. It

[15]

was a rotten job, but I was proud to be doing it for my father.

"I'm not surprised," was all my mother said.

We went to Playland only once that summer, and Dale went with us. When it was time to climb on the horses, Dad didn't get on at all; he went back to the car to wait for us. After one ride, Dale and I agreed the horses were too tame and used our string of tickets on the roller coaster.

When we got back to the car, Dad grinned and said "Get any gold rings?" He pushed a bottle under the seat.

"Ten of 'em," I answered quickly. I don't know why I didn't tell him about the roller coaster. By the time we got home, driving much too fast, it seemed too late to admit it.

The year I was fifteen, I almost fell in love. Althea was quiet and shy, which made her different from the other girls, who giggled and chattered nonstop and really put a guy off. There were the usual boy and girl get-togethers, but it took me almost two months of dreaming and planning to get up the nerve to ask Althea to go out with me alone.

One noon at school I blurted out an invitation to the show on Friday night.

"Pick you up at seven-thirty, okay?" I said quickly, before she could change her mind.

My problem—in addition to the problems of what I was going to talk to Althea about all evening and picking a show she'd really like, and deciding whether or not we should hold hands—was getting help from my parents. I wasn't driving yet and neither were my friends.

"I think that's fine," my mother said proudly, when I brought it up. As if I'd proved something by asking a girl out.

"Taking after his old man," Dad added. He fixed himself another drink and went to watch TV while Mom started banging around the kitchen. I could tell the vibes weren't too good, hadn't been all week. Dad had been sullen, and Mom made constant swiping remarks that he didn't pay attention to. But it didn't have anything to do with me. I had my own thing going for Friday.

On Friday, Dad came home from work, slamming down a box of papers and stuff with such a crash that both Mom and I jumped. Her eyes looked scared.

"Old Toothy Buscombe!" he shouted. "Screw his old job!"

"You've lost your job," my mother said. The words didn't come out excited, or surprised, or sympathetic or anything. Just words. I got the sinkingest feeling in my life.

Dad was still ranting as he opened the cupboard and got down a half-gallon of gin. He was buying bigger bottles now. Mom's eyes filled with tears and she turned her back on us.

"He tried to read me the riot act," Dad was saying, swallowing as fast as he was talking. "I'm way ahead of him. Told him before he could fire me, I'd quit. They'll be a while finding someone to fill my desk."

He poured the gin straight. All of a sudden I could see my whole evening with Althea falling to pieces. Dad wouldn't be able to drive me, and Mom would argue and get all shaky. With their own problems, they'd forget all about mine. I wanted to slam a few things myself.

Drinking had always made my dad conversational, teasing, joking, so I knew it wasn't the liquor that was making him so mad. I began developing a personal hatred for Toothy Buscombe, whom I didn't know, but who was deliberately hurting all of us.

I wasn't hungry at dinner. Finally I said, "I guess going to the show is off."

"You bet not!" Dad bellowed. "I'll take you and your girl to the show."

"I'll drive them," my mother said. That set Dad off

again, and he slammed his fork down on the plate and got up from the table. Picking up the half-empty bottle, he went to sit in the living room.

"Holler when you're ready, Julius," he called.

When I'd cleaned up, I came back to the living room. Dad jumped up. Mom got up too and hurried into her coat. As Dad and I started out the door, she was right with us. That really cooked it! I didn't have to be driven to pick up Althea with *both* parents, but I didn't know how to tell them.

I don't remember much about the show. I remember sitting with Althea beside me, trying to laugh when everyone else laughed, but my mind was home, imagining what was going on there, wondering if we could get through the evening without something terrible happening.

Mom was alone when she picked us up, and at Althea's door I just mumbled something and took off. When we got back to our house, Dad had gone to bed.

"She's a sweet girl," Mom said.

"I guess Dad's pretty upset about the job." I had to talk about the one important thing on my mind.

"It wasn't too much of a surprise."

"But Mom, what's he going to do now?"

She put away her coat and purse before answering. "I don't know, Julius. We'll think of something."

"Mom," I said, trying to hold her eyes but not succeeding. "He doesn't have to be this way. There's doctors and places. You've got to make him quit . . ."

Not saying the word aloud made it a little easier, less final—not that I didn't know the word, but I had already pushed it down in my mind. How could he be a lush, a drunk, an alcoholic? He was my father.

Gold Rings

"We can't do it for him, Julius. I can't talk him into anything. He doesn't listen; he doesn't want to hear. He has to do it himself. Maybe he'd hear you, but till then we'll do the best we can. Don't you worry about it."

That didn't answer anything. If he had to do it himself, he wouldn't listen to me either. And we'd just gotten so used to pretending that, well, yes, he drank a little, sometimes a little too much, but it wasn't all that serious. Except about the job, and that had me worried plenty.

It wasn't till a long time later that I even got around to thinking about Althea. Then I wasn't sure that I even liked her anymore.

A lot of things happened during the next two years. For a while Dad sat around and he didn't seem to be drinking much, but then I wasn't around much, so I couldn't be sure. Then one day he went to the clinic and from there to the hospital. While he was gone, we sold our house and found a smaller one in another neighborhood. I was pretty sick about it, but I decided my best contribution was just to shut up. I got work in the stockroom of a discount store on Saturdays and made a little money and stayed out of the house most of the time.

By the time Dad came home I'd had driver's training and Dale and Kevin and I had gotten our licenses. That way we were seeing more of each other. It was easier than ever to get out.

Most of the year just before I was seventeen was a good year. Dad got another job and was pretty straight arrow. I was busy with school and I had a girl I was really wild about, Kathy. Her house, with three younger sisters, was always a bunch of laughs. I was there a lot.

Kathy and I graduated together that June. I got a job with the Highway Department for the summer, repainting yellow lines with a crew on the Sierra Coast Freeway, and Kathy worked for an old lady who couldn't get around very well. We were going to junior college together in the fall.

Then Dad started drinking again, just a little, usually on weekends. I tried to convince myself it was nothing much, anyway, nothing like it had been a couple of years ago. Besides, I could ignore a lot of things. I was usually bushed at night and I spent a lot of time at Kathy's.

A few days before my eighteenth birthday, Mom asked me if I wanted anything special, like tickets to something or a special dinner. I told her my friends and I were going to Playland that night.

My birthday was a hot August day. Dad was sitting at the kitchen table, drinking a gin and tonic and making out an expense voucher. He'd poured a drink for Mom, which she sipped slowly. He even offered me one, and I guess he was disappointed because I didn't say yes.

"You're going to Playland tonight," Dad said, and I saw a funny expression on his face. It looked a little like envy.

"Yeah, you know, Kathy and Dale and Ann. Ann's crazy about the roller coaster—screams her head off," I said conversationally, avoiding mention of the merry-go-round.

"You kids never grow up, do you?" He got up and fixed another drink, and Mom's face suddenly closed up.

"It's kind of freaky when you're our age to swing on swings and teeter-totter and ride . . . on rides," I laughed.

"Go on a couple for your old dad," he said.

Then, because he kind of seemed to expect it, I added, "If I get the gold ring, I'll bring it home to you."

I showered and dressed. When I came back to the

kitchen, I heard Dad: "Have a good time tonight, huh, Julius? You deserve it, Son."

I walked into the living room. He was flopped in a chair.

"I'm proud of you," he said. "You give your dad a lot of pleasure, not like some kids."

He leaned forward, almost lost his balance. I put my hands out to steady him. I could feel the weight of his body. He was still big, but not the same kind of big he had once been. There were fat pouches now where there had been muscles. Unexpectedly, he caught my head between his hands, pulled me to him. I tried not to pull back from his breath.

"Do something for your old dad, Julius?" He fumbled in his pocket, pulled out a handful of bills. "Drive to the store—just take you a minute—pick up a fifth for me, huh, Julius?"

I shook my head slowly. "Can't, Dad."

"C'mon, Julius. You're a good son. Just that little thing. You kids got ways of doing it—identity card and things. Your dad knows some things. You're going out to have a good time. I wanna sit here and toast your birthday."

I wondered if I'd ever refused him anything before. It hurt to do it.

"No way, Dad. I've got to go."

He dropped his hand, exposing the old wrinkled burn scar on his arm, and let the bills fall to the floor. Hypnotized, I watched them drift down, a scattering of green paper at our feet, the money for just one more bottle, just one more ride on his personal merry-go-round.

He'd let me down, but it wasn't much of a shocker anymore. I had let him down even more. Not just tonight, but dozens of other nights. I had let him think I idolized him, no matter what. I had let myself believe there was no problem, no serious problem, because I wanted to believe it. Mom had given him a million words, till he no longer listened. But I had given him no words at all.

I walked through the kitchen, seeing Mom's face, the familiar mask of disapproval. There was one more thing I had to ask.

"You love him, Mom? You still love him?"

"Yes, Julius, I love him."

"I wonder," I said, and went out the back door, pulling it shut behind me. I got into the car, turned the ignition key. As I backed out to the street, I saw my mother's sorrowed face at the window above the kitchen sink. Was it love that had made her quiet and blind and cold? Was it love that was making me the same way? Or had we been riding around and around and around with him for so long that we didn't even know how to get off?

"Sorry, Dad," I said out loud to the inside of the car. "There are no more gold rings, no more free rides. But I haven't got the guts to say it to you myself."

I was already too old to be only eighteen.

THE KING, MY FATHER

by John Gilgun

There is a place where doors slam, dishes rattle, women scream, fists fly, and children run away to hide. That place is South Boston, on a Saturday night, after the bars close. In that place, I am one of those children. My mother is one of those women. I am nine, and it is my father's fist that lashes out, striking anything within range.

We never used the word "alcoholic" in connection with my father. It was always, "The man drinks." But, after all, didn't everyone? Weren't we Irish? Weren't we working class? Is the earth round? Do birds fly?

My father was well liked, popular in the bars, a very funny man at parties (in that summer of frantic parties, with half the country coming back from our victories in Europe and the Pacific); but he was a terror at home. Still, you never said, "That man is an alcoholic." Or, "That man needs help." My mother could talk about Ray Milland in *The Lost Week-*

end, the big movie that year, but she was incapable of making a connection between the film and my father's own weekends. Her response was always, "There's nothing we can do."

On our mean street, which ended, characteristically, in a blind alley, no neighbors ever came to help, no matter how loudly you hollered. To come into a man's house to break up a brawl—well, it was something you just didn't do. The local parochial school was sometimes a refuge from the violence at home, but nuns and priests never helped either. In fact, the sin was your own if you could not honor you father, and it was up to you to confess it on Saturday afternoon. You never said, "I can't honor that drunken bum," and if you thought it you had committed another sin. To confess the thought was to admit it into consciousness, where it would take root like an influenza virus. So you were trapped there also, within the confines of your own mind. "Jesus honored Mary and Joseph, though Jesus, as the Son of God, was greater than either of them," Father Ryan told us. How old was I before I replied, "But my parents aren't Mary and Joseph."

Or did I ever say that at all? Wasn't it rather my brother Kevin, three years older than myself, with a smart mouth and the wiry intelligence of a potential Jesuit, who came out with that one? When I reflect on my older brother, it's to realize that, though my impulse was to run away when the fights began, he was always in the center of things, flailing away. I also recall that Kevin never won in any single direct confrontation with our father. How could he win out, at the age of twelve, against a full-grown man of—how old was my father then? Thirty? But Kevin could always retire from the field of battle to the bedroom we shared—a bedroom stacked high with comic books which reiterated one theme and one theme only: that super-heroes never lose. Whereas, our father could only retire to his own room to sleep it off, waking to a hangover and mental confusion. In that time and in that place, my brother and I dreamed of our father's downfall.

Then the war ended. The lights were on again all over the world. We had gone oom-pah, oom-pah right in the Führer's face. There were bluebirds over the white cliffs of Dover. And the future was ours. Doors were opening on corridors which had been sealed off for centuries and many things seemed possible which had never seemed possible before.

And back into our world came our mother's younger brother, David—a war hero with an honest-to-God leg wound and medals which he modestly kept in his dresser drawer. He had gone off to war five years before, cocky and self-assured, like Jimmy Cagney in *Yankee Doodle Dandy*, a pint-sized loudmouth from the back streets of Southie. But he was returning a man, a hero, with a new humility and the conviction that the world would now be made safe for something or other.

Kevin and I, leaning on the windowsill in the parlor, watched as he walked toward our house, down that grim street, using his cane. "That's him!" Kevin cried. "That's David. *Now* you'll see some changes around this old place, wait and see!"

David was living with his parents (that is, our maternal grandparents) until he could get settled, get a job, find a place of his own. The newspapers and magazines were full of articles that summer about problems of adjustment experienced by returning servicemen, particularly those who had been wounded in action. Now that I'm older than David was in 1945, I realize that he must have experienced these problems, but neither Kevin nor I was aware of them then.

People were being cautioned about pressuring veterans into getting jobs too quickly. David had no job, so it must have been a rootless time for him. He took us everywhere—to the zoo, to the beach, to parades. He also spent a great deal of time at our house. He was our mother's favorite brother and my father liked him, even though David did not drink.

One of the images which comes back to me from that time is of David's cane resting against the back of the booth in the corner bar and grill. My father and mother are drinking beer, but David is drinking Coke with Kevin and me. You proved your manhood by drinking alcohol (I understood that from an early age), but David didn't need to prove it. His wound proved it for him. My father's arm is on David's shoulder and my father is saying, "I didn't like you when you went away. Thought you were a piss-ass kid. But I like you now. I like you now." My brother is playing with a swizzle stick. His eyes are on David and they shine with a peculiar intensity.

Now, I wonder, did my brother have a well-thought-out plan? Was he capable of that at age twelve? Or was he merely chancing it when he said things like, "David, our father is a regular Hitler around our house. Look at the bruises on my arms." Or, "My father is no good. I wish I had *you* for a father." Or, "If I had a sister and I loved her, I wouldn't let her husband beat her the way our father beats our mother."

I participated sometimes by confirming what he said, but I don't remember contributing much original material myself. No, the conflict was between Kevin, the firstborn, and our father. Only years later, when I discovered the works of Freud, did I begin to understand this intellectually. At any rate, David's eyes and ears could tell him that things were not right in our house. A meal that passed without an argument, an evening that passed without some violent altercation—these were rare. But how often my brother precipitated the arguments! And almost always, I realize now, for David's benefit.

Then, one hot night after a particularly unpleasant set-to, during which our mother had fled the house after being slapped (followed by David, who had now seen it all himself), my brother laughed in the privacy of our bedroom and told me, "*Now* you'll see something! Just wait!" But it had been my brother who had started it all by humming a song called "Drunk Last Night, Drunk the Night Before" at the dinner table and by staring at our father in a provocative, contemptuous way while he did it.

"Wake up! They're going to fight!"

Kevin shook me, woke me out of a deep sleep, and hustled me down the hall to the partially open kitchen door. Before my eyes adjusted to the chink of light, I was aware of what was happening because I heard David shouting at my father. They were together there in the kitchen, facing each other.

"Kids talk, Frank!" I heard him say. "You can't keep things from kids. I know you beat my sister all the time. What did I see tonight? Did you hit her tonight? Is she hiding out at some friend's house because you hit her tonight?"

"Ah, when you're married, David, you'll understand. Come and talk to me then. It's not as simple as you think! But what do you know anyway? You're just a kid!"

"I know more than you think. And when I get through with you tonight, you're going to know it, too. Do you want to have it out here or do you want to fight in the yard? I can take you, Frank. You know I can. And tonight you're going to get what you've earned."

"You won't hit a man in his own house."

"Then come outside with me. Come outside and fight like the man you pretend to be!"

"David," my father said, "I won't hit a cripple."

"One little shrapnel wound isn't going to keep me from teaching a lesson to a son of a bitch like you! I fight with my hands, not my legs!"

In spite of the years that have passed since then, I remember the high excitement and tension of that scene—the two men circling each other around the table in that lighted room, my older brother kneeling beside me at the door, his hand around my waist . . . and then our father, suddenly charming and ingratiating, saying, "Let's talk this over, David. Let's have a drink on it. I know you don't drink, but you can't refuse a glass of good Irish whiskey with your own brother-in-law at a time like this."

"I won't drink with you!"

"Of course you will, David. You'll drink with me out of respect for me, because I'm older and I'm your brother-in-law. And then I'll tell you why I had to marry your sister, and what it's been like for me in this house in the last twelve and a half years with her and Kevin. I ruined my life by doing the right thing."

How long did Kevin and I lean there, peering through that opening, taking it all in? How long did the two men drink? And how much of Kevin's adult life—his own alcoholism, the failure of two marriages—was prefigured in what he heard? Sometimes, even now, I find myself waking from a dream of that final scene. I see David, unused to alcohol, leaning slightly forward in his chair, the glass between his hands. I see our father moving menacingly up behind him, saying, "Oh, you'll learn, son! They told you that life is something wonderful and glorious, but you'll learn. It's nothing but shit, and you'll learn that. It's a job you hate, a wife who can't respect you, kids who torment you day and night. It's poverty and dirt and injustice. You have a hell of a lot to learn!"

Then he raised his fist and brought it down as hard as he could on the vulnerable, exposed spot at the base of David's skull. The blow propelled David forward toward the door behind which we were hiding. The glass crashed on the edge of the kitchen sink. My brother, who had already been crying, shouted, "No!" and threw himself forward at our father. Taken by surprise, he fell backward under Kevin's thrust. It was the first time Kevin had ever managed to topple him, and I believe it did more to change my father's life than any other single thing which ever happened in that household.

My father was institutionalized at the age of fifty-seven, and he died in a state hospital in Massachusetts six years later. At the wake, both my brother and myself refused to touch alcohol. Later I heard that one of our cousins commented on this, saying: "I always thought there was something odd about those two."

THE GENIE IN THE BOTTLE

by Rebecca Blackwell

Days are divided into parts. They have to be in order for me to survive. There is the morning part, so often fervently wished for—cups of coffee after the kids have left for school, sunlight, and the pleasant perception that everything is really all right after all. The enraged monster that broke the dishes and threatened to kill me in the dark hours of last night has receded into the shadows and been replaced by the man I married.

Days progress from morning. It becomes afternoon and soon the kids come racing in, faces bright with laughter and apples in their cheeks from the crisp October air. Terry does a mock karate stance as he nears the kitchen. This is his latest love. Maureen hastens to tell me that she has been chosen to draw the autumn picture on the school bulletin board.

Children are remarkable creatures. Their resilience amazes me. Looking at the freckled, laughing faces, I'm convinced, for the moment at least, that they're growing up all right after all. Several of the blackberry tarts I've baked disappear, and they're off to play.

Five o'clock approaches and I start supper. The potatoes are peeled and the stew meat is browning in the pan. There are a few carrots left in the garden that I might as well pull. In the woods across the street, the sun is just beginning to dip behind the trees. For the eleven years that I've lived here, I've loved this place more than any I've ever known. I can remember Terry and me sitting outside long before the garden was planted—before the house was even finished—and dreaming of how it would look someday. "Time to come in now," I call to Terry and Maureen, playing kickball in the deserted street.

At six-thirty young Terry, in the den watching the sports news, asks, "Has Daddy called?" It is not the same voice I heard earlier. It is somehow older. Maureen continues to color a picture at the kitchen table. The tight feeling in my stomach, an old and familiar companion in the evenings, begins to grow.

At seven I decide there's no point in ruining supper for everyone, so I serve the kids and myself. As though trying to shake off the heavy atmosphere, the kids are acting increasingly silly. It's harmless enough, but it gets on my nerves and I finally holler at them to stop it. Maureen helps me clear off the dishes, giving me her best seven-year-old toothless smile. Hugging her, I apologize for hollering. "Don't worry, Mommy," she says, but doesn't look convincing.

I jump at the phone's ring at five minutes to eight. It's always like that in the evening when Terry's out.

"It's for you, Mommy," Terry says. "Some lady from the hospital."

It turns out to be a nurse from the emergency room of our local hospital. Years ago she and her ex-husband used to double date with Terry and me.

"Terry's here, Linda. . . . No, he's not badly hurt . . . but he's been in an accident. He's got some facial lacerations that he won't let us treat." Her voice sounds odd and embarrassed. "You know, Linda, second opinion and all that. . . . He wants you to look at them first and okay it."

I feel ashamed as I picture what's going on at the hospital.

"That's ridiculous, Carol. I—I haven't got a car. I'd have to get a cab."

After I hang up, the significance of not having a car, and all its implications, hits me full force. Our car—just bought two months before—what about the car? But then I realize what I'm doing. I'm acting more concerned about the car than I am about Terry. There is a numbness, after a while, to going through the many brushes with death that are part and parcel of life with an alcoholic. She said he was all right, didn't she? He'll wait, by God, just as I've waited so often. At eight-twenty, Carol calls again, sounding more impatient and pressured this time. A neighbor agrees to give me a ride to the hospital and watch the kids.

In the emergency room Terry is lying on a treatment table, several gauze sponges on his face soaking up blood. He's crying and obviously drunk. When he realizes it's me he grows angry, asking where in the hell I've been. The young intern and nurses all seem to be staring, and I find my face growing warm with embarrassment. Terry's voice has an odd nasal quality. The doctor removes one of the sponges to reveal a long, deep slash across the bridge of Terry's nose.

"I've been telling your husband that this laceration

needs to be sutured, Mrs. Connors, but he won't believe me," the intern tells me angrily.

"He's right, Terry," I venture. "Now, let him fix that cut—"

"Fuck you, Linda, you would agree with him. You'd agree with anything that's against me." The monster that comes out of a bottle in the evenings is here now in the emergency room.

"Well, I think we've wasted enough time, Mr. Connors," the intern says through clenched teeth. "Carol, get some more help and fifty milligrams of Thorazine."

Five of us—yes, I help—hold my husband down while giving the tranquilizer time to work. He's begun to cry again.

"I'm sorry, Linda, I'm so sorry. I've fucked the car all up." Gradually he calms down, and the gashes are closed with sutures. He'll have scars, I realize.

"I think it's best we keep him overnight, Mrs. Connors, just to be sure he doesn't have a concussion," the doctor says. There is no mention of observation for the drinking problem he does have. "X rays were negative for skull fracture," he continues, "but of course he does have a fractured cheek, and the nose. . . ."

"Well, I did it again, didn't I?" he asks me as I walk beside the stretcher taking him upstairs. "The Waynesboro police found me walking along the highway . . . I—I don't even remember the accident. Linda, I don't even know where the car is."

"You're alive, that's the important thing. We'll find out about the car tomorrow." My voice sounds harder than I want it to.

"You'd be better off if I'd been killed," Terry groans. He's starting to cry again, and I know I should say something comforting, but I can't. The silence between us, broken only by the whir of the stretcher wheels along the polished tile floor, is deafening. As I say good night, Terry grabs my hand.

"God, Linda, you don't wish I'd died, do you?"

With remarkable clarity I realize an unsuspected truth. Tears sting my eyes, but there's a strange peace in acknowledging it.

"Yes, Terry, I guess I'd just as soon you did die, if you're going to keep drinking this way. What's the difference? Only that this way you're killing yourself and everything around you slowly. . . ."

Later, sitting in the darkness of the den, I smoke a cigarette in the middle of the night. It is nothing new to me. I've done it a thousand nights while Terry slept, oblivious to everything with the help of the genie in the bottle. This is a time for thinking about tomorrow. Tomorrow everything will be all right again. Tomorrow I'll take the kids and leave . . .

The knotty pine walls are warm in the dim light. Terry loves wood—he's a good craftsman. We put these walls up, board by board. Terry and I—turning over the garden in spring, walking in the woods, laughing, building this house.

Must I throw away the good because of the genie in the bottle? There have been times he's tried to stop but somehow just couldn't. Sometimes I think that maybe he's crazy, but more often I wonder if I am. The articles that I read call me and all the other people like me passive-aggressive and masochistic, but they don't mention love, that intangible that makes me doubt my sanity. If he's sick, would he be less sick if I left him? Maybe he would, if the magazine articles are right. The shock just might do the trick. But what if it doesn't?

There it is, as plain as the nose on your face, dummy, there's the gamble. Take the losses and brief moments of happiness that life with an alcoholic—one you love—affords you, or go for broke.

Pajama-clad young Terry, a freckle-faced miniature of his father, tiptoes into the room. "I came down for a drink of water. . . . I wasn't sleeping anyway. Is Daddy all right?"

Assured that Daddy's fine and will be out of the hospital tomorrow, his ten-year-old cherub's face still looks worried. "Mommy, you're not going to get a divorce from Daddy like you told him the other night, are you?"

Caught off guard, I simply reply, "I don't know."

"Please don't, Mommy. I'd miss him and I bet he'd be lonesome, too. You said yourself he's sick."

I have no answers. I smile my best smile and say, "Don't worry, sweetheart, you go to sleep now." I can't think anymore—the dilemma is too much for me. I'll go to sleep now, too. Maybe in the morning, in the sunlight, I'll be able to see things better.

JOHN GARDNER AND THE SUMMER GARDEN
by Catherine Petroski

Tonight I am holding my nose.

To talk to John Gardner.

He will answer the pay phone at the end of the bar at Gardner Gardens. I will ask him if my father is there because my mother wants to know but is tired and ashamed of calling the tavern herself. John Gardner will say, "Just a minute and I'll see," and then he'll put his hand over the phone for a second and come back and say, "No, I don't see him," and then still holding my nose like a long-distance operator and sounding stuck-up I will say, "Thank you, sir," and wait until he hangs up and then hang up myself, while my father is saying, "Thank you, John. I gotta be going."

Every night one of my jobs is to call Gardner Gardens. I can count on it. Weekdays, weekends, my father will be there when it's time for supper. At first it was fun, sort of, but now I can see why Mother doesn't want to call anymore, why she gave me the job. So for a long time now, I have been a different person every night. By now John Gardner must be pretty confused about why my father gets so many phone calls from so many different people.

What we all understand, Mother and Father and I, is that it's just a signal. We all know he's there. There's never any question. John Gardner's saloon is only two blocks from our house and I used to ride my bike down to see if Father was really there, and he was. There are lots of saloons in town but if he went to another one it would just get all complicated. This way Father finds out when dinner is ready without starting a real fight about where he was hanging out. This way it's all in the neighborhood. John Gardner's tavern is down the hill past the Catholic church, just on the other side, in fact. The tavern has beer signs that work like magic and whiskey that nobody ever drinks and is full of the smell of old spilled beer and cigarettes. Out in back is a little fake brick building that's really one big barbecue pit inside. In the summer John Gardner's wife sells barbecued ribs and pork sandwiches there. And root beer and orange. There's a summer garden, too, all screens, which they say is why it's called Gardner Gardens. In the summer John Gardner carries out beer in sloshy pitchers. I don't see how anybody drinks beer. It tastes like soap. I hate it.

Tonight, when I told Mother what John Gardner had said, she gave the lima beans a good, mean stir. "That man would lie to his own mother," she said, "if it meant selling another beer." She picked up the telephone and asked the operator for the number I had just called. But she hung up before John Gardner had had a chance to answer.

"Those front legs don't amount to much," Father said,

looking at the pieces of squirrel on my plate. "What's the matter? Not hungry?"

He was trying to be nice, trying to make little jokes and be happy the way he does when he knows Mother's mad or he's stayed a little too long at Gardner's, which happens every once in a while. Mother doesn't think he's funny. I laugh a little to make him feel better and Mother stares at me.

"What's so funny?" she says.

"Daddy's funny." I don't know why I call him Daddy sometimes. He's Father.

"It's the beer, and that's not one bit funny," Mother says. "You'd think a person would try to get home when he's expected. After all I've gone through with the squirrels."

"Have to chase them down, Lou?" he asks. I giggle.

"You know what I mean. It's barely civilized."

"It was good enough for the pioneers," Father says.

"And the cavemen," I start to say, but Mother interrupts me.

"Well, it's ready," she says.

Dumb John Gardner, I think. Why does he have to go and sell Father all that beer that starts the trouble? What's so interesting about that smelly place with all those loud men? Daddy takes a head off the platter and puts it on his plate first thing.

"Now, this'll put hair on your chest," he says to me. He pries off the lower jaw and the little teeth glisten in their gravy bath. The big cutting teeth stay with the eyeless skull.

"Here," he says to me, and he puts the tongue on my plate next to the beans I wasn't planning to eat. It is a very small tongue. Mine grows fat in my mouth.

Father steadies the skull at the middle of his plate. The head is bare now. The cover of meat is gone.

"That's a good knife you've got there," Mother says and hands him another, an old one from the clubhouse. With the handle, Father cracks the case in one short blow and removes the brain.

"You can have the next one," he says to Mother.

"No thanks," she says, and she eats a forkful of mashed potatoes. I study the broken head on the edge of Father's plate. There are holes that were its nose.

The siren woke me up. Too low for the police, too high for the ambulance. It must be Snow White, the little white fire truck from the Twelfth Street substation. It stopped somewhere near. Then there were other sirens, police, the big trucks from downtown, an ambulance. It sounded like just down the street from us. I got out of bed.

Mother was flapping around in her scuffs and robe. Father was getting dressed. "What can you do?" Mother kept asking. "Don't you think you're just going to be in the way?" Father kept getting dressed.

"Where is it? The Catholic school?" I wanted to know.

"Don't know," my father said. "It's somewhere close. My God, Lou. Look at the sky."

We looked and it was pink with smoke and light.

"You're being ridiculous. You're going to get hurt. You've got no business going down there. What can you do? You're just going to be in the way. Don't go. Please don't go." He was halfway off the front porch by then and just turned and yelled, "You stay here, now."

"Don't get close," Mother called after him.

I sat on the landing, afraid but wishing I could go too.

"Back to bed," she ordered. She turned and went to the kitchen.

In the morning it was as though nothing had happened. Father was eating his two slices of toast with damson plum jam and drinking his tomato juice and black coffee, reading the paper, not saying anything. My toast was waiting and already cold. "Tavern Gutted by Fire," the headline read. I could see it from my chair. Gardner's saloon was gone, just like that. The forever-falling waterfalls, the bounding spots of red and yellow and blue, the scenes of the North Woods lit from the back, the Southern swamps with their droopy trees. Destroyed, probably. And no place anymore for the loud music on the jukebox, and women smoking at the tables, slopping beer from pitcher to glass and from glass to mouth and maybe to the front of a dress, and yelling at kids whose noses needed wiping and whose hair was not combed and whose shoes were untied. The bad women, Father called them. The smell of spilled beer and stale smoke was gone, and now the new smoke.

My bike-horse, Trigger, was damp with dew. I had left it outside leaning against the back porch. I had forgotten again to put it in the garage and if I rode away quickly they might not notice. The heavy smell of smoke and water hung all around. Through the schoolyard, up the hill. In everybody's open windows.

All that was left of John Gardner's was the remains of the brick walls and mounds of soggy junk. A man I had never seen before poked through the junk. The smell was awful.

The summer garden was safe. The giant cottonwoods and catalpas that surrounded it had been curled back by the fire, but the beer garden itself was the same as always. The paper Japanese lanterns caught a bit of the morning sun, and the pale colors danced in the east wind. I leaned Trigger against the side of the summer garden.

The screen door creaked. Along the walls stood the tables

and benches. The summer jukebox was in place. I heard a stray cat stirring.

The stray cat turned out to be John Gardner. He was lying on his back on one of the benches. "What are you doing here?" he asked.

"Nothing. Just looking around."

"Everybody's looking," John Gardner said. "Not much to see, is there?"

I agreed. I told him I was sorry his tavern got burnt up. I wasn't sorry in one way, but I didn't tell him that. But in another way I was sorry because we could always count on Father's being at Gardner's. So I said just that we were sorry, especially Father, I guessed.

"I know," John Gardner said and coughed a little. He sat up on the bench and lit a Lucky. "That's right," he said as if he'd just remembered something. "That's right, you're the one's always calling for your pa to come home and eat."

"No," I lied.

But he stayed silent, his blue eyes distant. Old John Gardner wasn't even as old as Father. I could see him with the phone, tilting his yellow head to one side, going to Father, holding up one hand flat and pointing in its palm to the direction of the phone. I turned for the screen door.

"Hey, don't run off," he said. I looked back and felt very sorry for him. Now that the saloon was gone, what would he do? What would any of us do?

"I got a joke for you," he said. Sometimes Father brought home jokes with the homemade horseradish he got from somebody at John Gardner's. But Mother wouldn't let him finish the stories.

"That's okay," I told him. "I wouldn't get it anyway.' Or so Mother always said.

"It's a clean joke, kind of," John Gardner said kindly.

"You'll get it. You're the only one who might."

"Well, okay. Tell me."

John Gardner's face broke into a fat smile, the biggest smile anybody ever saw. With the hand that held the Lucky, he pinched his nose between his thumb and his fourth finger.

"Gardner Gardens," he said.

And we both laughed and laughed.

Drinkers and
Their Stories

RUNNING

by David Adams

Penelope is pregnant. Never has she been so healthy. Never has she felt so good. No drinks for her anymore—she doesn't need them. (Bruce says she is as happy as a clam with the disposition of a contented cow.)

What is happening to Bruce in front of Penelope's very eyes? Is he crumbling? How does she feel about it? Maybe, for her, this is a movie. Penelope sees Bruce come home and go quickly to the kitchen for his first drink of the evening. She wakes him in the evening when he passes out in front of the television set. "Are you all right?" she asks when he wakes up in the middle of the night and pads out to the kitchen for another drink. He pats her thigh reassuringly.

One night Bruce's stomach catches fire. Pepto-Bismol doesn't help. Bruce just knows he is in the last stages of cancer. The pain grows worse and worse. At two A.M. he orders a cab. He doesn't dare drive to the hospital emergency ward. Penelope goes with him.

HAVING BEEN THERE

Bruce waits an hour for the intern to examine him. The intern says, "You have been drinking too much—you have gastritis. Now, if you want to go to Alcoholics Anonymous meetings, we have them every Tuesday night here at the hospital." Bruce doesn't argue with the doctor, he knows better than that. He figures the doctor smelled liquor on his breath and jumped to a conclusion.

The bad times are coming more frequently now. When Bruce gets up in the morning he says he can't possibly make it to work. He is too frightened, too shaky, too miserable. One day he is also out of liquor.

Penelope asks, "Do you want me to walk down and get you some more?" She doesn't drive. She knows Bruce won't want to be seen outside.

"But it's too early," Bruce says, "too damned early."

"I know," Penelope says, "But later?"

"Bar's open," Bruce says. "Will you ride with me down to the bar?"

Penelope throws on a housecoat and they drive four blocks and angle-park. Bruce walks into the bar quickly. Double Corby's and water. Poured right to the brim. He can't pick it up without spilling it. The barmaid is busy. He can't ask the guy next to him to pour it. He lowers his head to get his mouth closer to the shot glass. He manages to throw most of the drink into his mouth. He brushes the whiskey drops off his bristly cheek. In a panic he finally gets the barmaid's eye and gets a fill-up.

They go back to the apartment, and later in the morning Penelope says, "Do you need more?"

"Oh, I don't know," he says. He avoids her eyes. He thinks, Well, if I'm going to miss work today anyway, a few

[46]

drinks can't hurt. Of course, if I drink too much today, I won't get to work tomorrow either.

"Yeah, yeah," Bruce says, "why don't you. Yeah. Go pick up a jug."

Penelope knows that at this point she is an instrument. She wants to help. She is not quite sure how to help. She goes into the bedroom to dress.

"Twenty fucking minutes already," Bruce says to himself. "Twenty fucking minutes. Jesus Christ."

He lights a cigarette. "Will you be all right until I get back?" Penelope asks.

"I think so," Bruce says, and takes a long drag. Penelope takes five more minutes to find her purse, and by this time Bruce is in the bathroom. He hears the screen door slam.

He walks into the kitchen and pulls last night's bottle out of the wastebasket. He tries to suck one more drop from it.

Two weeks in Resort City on the new job. In TV. Fresh from Indianapolis, back East. Where all their friends were. The trip from Indiana to Resort City a bitch. Car piled high with odds and ends the moving company didn't take. Penelope's mammoth wall mural (in process) filling the entire back end of the car to within one inch of the back of Bruce's neck. Siamese cat, Shazzam, on the top of the painting, yowling every inch of the way.

Mississippi River one hell of a long way down. Bruce shook to pieces. Five beers on the other side before his nerves got calm enough to drive again.

Kansas in 1959 before superhighways. Depressing. Monotonizing. Up and down, up and down. The wind tore at the car, trying to wrench it off the highway. Bruce fought back, knuckles sore.

The coldest night in Colby, Kansas. All night long the wind blew hard. The end of the world and no going back. The loose screen door on the motel unit smacked and rattled. Bruce knew he had sailed out to the edge. Point of no return.

By the time Bruce and Penelope reached Resort City, he was nearly out of gas and it was achingly cold. Two days later he was virtually out of money, too. He had made a $100 error in the checking account, and Penelope had made a $250 error on their tax return.

Resort City once was a dream. When he had spent a two-hour layover there on his way to Army camp in World War II, Bruce had vowed to come back. Come back he did after college for about six months. He'd lived in a rooming house fairly close to the downtown area, close enough to walk to his job when he couldn't afford the bus fare. The sun's hot glare was tempered by trees lining the streets.

There was no insulation from the sun now, in an apartment on the edge of town in the sand and the rocks. Icy winds in the winter. One Sunday morning Bruce and Penelope drove to the spot Bruce remembered where he had tried to wrestle the virginity from a Virginia gentlewoman. Now the waterfall trickled instead of roared, the grass was dried, the park bench broken.

Penelope walks now to the drugstore that sells liquor. She worries about Bruce, but not constantly. She feels detached, not really part of the situation. Sometimes Penelope worries about herself. But not like in the old days. She feels too good. What happens to Bruce is a *film*. You laugh. You cry. You dab at your eyes. You walk down the street and buy a dish of ice cream.

The big show, the real show, is happening inside Penelope. She is duplicating herself, but with a difference. With all the hurts and faults removed, all slings and arrows conveniently disposed of. She is giving birth to herself defect-free. (There is a sad man who lives in my house, says Penelope, and when he goes out, I wave to him. He drives down the street and disappears. I walk into the bedroom and lie down and I feel with my hands the wonder of me inside of me and I close my eyes and dream.)

The telephone rings. Bruce wonders what to do. If he is sick, really, really sick, how can he answer the telephone? Assuming it's someone from the office. But if he is really sick, how come his wife would leave him and not be there to answer the telephone? Could he say he had gone to the doctor? Not this early, probably. Better answer, better answer—he put his weak voice on: "Hello."

They hang up.

What a job to go back to, Bruce thinks. What a job. The first day his office had been piled high with papers. One of the girls was doing double duty and resenting it. On top of that she was ugly and compensated by remembering the hateful details of other people's lives: the fact that one engineer was a secret drinker, that another's wife was suing him for divorce. Gertrude was her name. Gertrude had an immense nose. And a medicated odor, as if she were applying a shrinking compound to this enormous appendage.

Sweet William was what Bruce called Gertrude's boss. His perfectly waved hair looked fresh from the hairdresser. His sonorous voice carried an authority and conviction unrelated to quality of intellect or personal attractiveness.

Sweet William was a living prototype of the Ken doll, a number of years before the Barbie cult surfaced. It was his position as sales-service manager Bruce was supposed to move into so that Sweet William could devote more time to new duties. But somehow he had Bruce outmaneuvered. Bruce never figured out quite why, but he could never lay a glove on him.

Will Penelope ever come back? Bruce hurts all over. The breakfast drink has worn off. He hears the music. He turns off the radio switch, but the music keeps coming. He hears the masses, the masses that sweep down from the summit of the mountain on the high and howling wind. The ever-moan of the mass winds ushers in the end. He knows there isn't much time left—the world has used up its chances. His dreams are tearing flesh and fire now. The bombs are about to drop. THE BOMB. It doesn't matter. If you knew what Bruce knew, you'd drink, too. He is living through the last days of the world, and his superior sensitivity feels every last vibration the world is making in its death agony. A drink? A small thing. God bless its warm blossom in my empty belly, cries Bruce. One more good feeling before the world disintegrates. Could you deny so small a pleasure?

Penelope returns. (Blare of trumpets.) She marches in with the Most High Anointment. He sloshes the whiskey in a tumbler. He drinks it off. He chases it with water. He holds the bottle to the sunlight, rejoicing in the golden glow so like a church window from some fond memory. Now Bruce can calmly walk because today is taken care of. He is not going to work. He is ill. He is recuperating. He will be in excellent shape tomorrow as long as he doesn't drink too much today. Today he is simply tapering off.

It is a gorgeous day. Soon the postman will come by. With good news? Perhaps a letter from a friend back at the Indianapolis TV station. And, by God, the mailman does putt-putt up on his three-wheeler—a little late but still—and delivers a delicious letter. Hilarious. And Bruce drags out his typewriter so he can write an even more hilarious letter back, telling them all about this squinty-assed place.

One day stretches to a few, and Bruce knows this paradise cannot last. He learns to play canasta with Penelope and drinks a lot of tea. It keeps his fingers busy and his mind occupied.

The television station has sent flowers. When Penelope called and mentioned the hospital emergency ward, it had been misinterpreted. Or Penelope had overdramatized. The flowers were forwarded to the apartment. And one of the salesmen dropped by to visit. And wish Bruce a speedy recovery.

The morning comes when it is time to go back to work. Bruce has not been drinking for several days. Still, he retches. He retches at the thought of going back to work. He does not want to face the light, the people. Nobody who retches like this should go to work. How can food stay down when a man is heaving like this? Should a man go to work on an empty stomach? Bruce forces down an eggnog and locks his jaws. He fights the convulsive heaves.

Bruce sits a minute and smokes his cigarette. It burns his raw throat.

"You going to be all right?" Penelope asks.

"Smiling, the boy fell dead."

Penelope smiles.

Bruce shakes gently now. Only an occasional heave to fight down. He swallows coffee. He pulls the muscles of his face into a smile. He says to himself, I am with my many months' pregnant wife, Penelope. We are sitting like a normal couple who are having an after-breakfast chat over coffee before Daddy-to-be goes to work to buy baby shoes. The sunshine in the kitchen bids me stay. But I won't. Today I will have enough courage to go.

Bruce gets up and puts on one pair of sunglasses. He puts another pair in his pocket. He must drive toward the east, toward the rising sun that blinds him. Some mornings he can see nothing but the side of the road. So Bruce always drives slowly. This angers other drivers. So Bruce puts on his *second* pair of sunglasses. That way he can make out the ghostly image of the car ahead. And follow it.

Bruce walks to the car and carefully inserts the key into the door lock. Carefully, because everything he does now is carefully. He has learned to modify his movements so that they appear to be the same whether he is drinking heavily or not. This means slowing down when he is sharp and speeding up when he is dull. Hoping to find some acceptable medium. But it doesn't always work. Just the other day there was a bluenose in the grocery store who warned his little girl, "Watch out for the drunk." Bruce felt mortified.

Bruce climbs into his car. Penelope stands out on the doorstep. She waves. She seems to like this tableau of happy domesticity—the waving wife, the husband driving away with a toot of the horn. Bruce knows that one day soon he will be coming back early. Too early. Because he is bringing an empty cargo. Because he will have been fired.

Now Bruce hardly ever feels really well. Some symptoms he can isolate. Asthma for one. Before he left Indianapolis he told everyone he was going to Resort City because it would be wonderful for his asthma. It didn't work out that way. Bruce has trouble breathing through his nose as well. Possibly because his capillaries expand from the drinking and cigarettes. Once he and Penelope visited a doctor, and Bruce was completely honest. "I drink a lot, Doctor," he said.

Running

"You have rhinosinusitis," the doctor said. "Do you hit your wife when you drink?"

"No, he is a lamb when he drinks," said Penelope. "He simply passes out." The doctor scribbled prescriptions for nose drops and tranquilizers.

Bruce is not always a lamb. He seethes a lot, inside. But what could he do with a pregnant wife? What could he do with anybody? Bruce is not good at expressing anger. Sometimes he boils over. He has slapped Penelope.

Once Bruce was driving along on a Saturday afternoon with a full head of booze when a pickup sideswiped his car. Bruce chased the truck down the street and through several alleys. When he finally caught up, the truck was in a parking lot behind a building. A dusty little dirt farmer climbed out.

"You want to go in?" asked the farmer. Bruce looked up and saw they had ended up at the rear of the police station. He knew he'd get locked up for a thousand years if he walked in smelling like booze.

"No," Bruce said, "but you are a lousy fucking driver. You got insurance?"

"No," said the farmer.

"Shit," said Bruce, and got back in his car.

Bruce makes it into work. He sits in the lopsided desk chair that somebody has salvaged from the Salvation Army. He starts to move through the accumulation of a week's work that has piled up on his desk. He tries to make sense out of commercial schedules. He *could* go to the canteen for a cup of coffee but thinks better of it. He doesn't need, doesn't like, doesn't *want* eyes. He doesn't want eyes watching his shaking hand spill the scalding coffee on his fingers. He doesn't want ears hearing the echo of his voice, the high, tight voice that anxiety squeezes from his vocal chords.

HAVING BEEN THERE

Franklin, the manager, pokes his head in the door. "How you doing?"

"Okay, now," Bruce says.

"What doctor you see?"

"Mmmm. Jesus, I can't recollect the name at the moment. Wow. I gotta take a crap. See you later." Franklin knew everybody in town.

Franklin isn't a bad guy. Tall, balding, white-haired, lean and tan, he gets along well with almost everybody. Sometimes he retreats to the program director's film lab for most of the day—Bruce suspects he's nursing a hangover. Sometimes when Bruce talks to Franklin there are phone calls that suggest that some of his evening business may be pleasant. Franklin is, quite simply, the kind of guy who makes the sales world go round. He knows the moves of the town's jet set, who is sleeping with whom, who just bought what new sports car, the football chatter, the baseball chatter, the whole jock and society matrix that makes most businessmen feel comfortable on their upward-mobility trip. Franklin himself had had his upward mobility interrupted by an unfortunate shaft from a major company back East. But he had landed on his feet in Resort City. Will I? Bruce wonders.

Bruce also works with Jane, the girl who prepares the traffic log, the girl who sometimes helps Bruce when he gets overwhelmed by work. She's kind and friendly. Cheerful, competent, attractive. Bruce wants to date her, only he isn't single anymore. And under too much of a strain anyway. Perhaps golf? They talk about it. But they don't get around to it.

Even on the best of days there is strain. Resort City TV is highly condensed compared to Indianapolis. For every four or five people back East there is one here.

Bruce keeps on pushing hard during the weeks he *is* working and creates some semblance of order. He tries to keep the accounts adequately serviced. He writes the day-to-day new commercials and the speculation commercials to help the salesmen land new accounts. He starts the mammoth job of clearing the files of outdated materials. He is careful not to throw away anything that might be needed again.

Later that morning, Franklin calls Bruce downstairs. (Will he give me the axe? Bruce wonders.) There, sitting with him, is the manager of the city's leading department store. He wants a test shot right away, and he's going to get it because Franklin has been busting his balls to get the store on the air. Bruce takes notes on the hosiery the manager has brought with him. He runs upstairs, types up a commercial, dashes down the hall, and delivers it over a call-letter slide from the announce booth. All in twenty minutes from notes to airtime.

With the kind of pace he's leading, Bruce doesn't spend much time talking to co-workers. The kids' show host stops by now and then. He's worked big-market TV and is in town for a year on personal business—his wife's father is going through a terminal illness. Tom has smarts. The other "talent" on the staff are predominantly conservative; Tom is a socialist, pacifist. One of the guys has a soft spot doing a fifteen-minute nightly right-wing diatribe for an oil company. His job—help keep America safe for oil-depletion allowances. Once Bruce tries to play softball on a Saturday morning with some of the staff. The sun is hellishly hot. Bruce hasn't played ball for fifteen years and it shows. He doesn't try that again.

Bruce has two friends from earlier days in the city. One, an apple-cheeked kid he worked with in Connecticut. Mike was as American as blueberry or apple pie and not a hell of a lot more interesting over the long haul. So conversation with him died fairly fast. Another friend, Bill Gass, was also a socialist and a poet and writer. But somehow "the thrill was gone" there, too. That old acquaintance wasn't worth much more than one beer-drinking evening. Bill was hot to save the world, but he got frightened fast when confronted with an individual going down for the third time.

Pressures? Bruce has plenty of them. Trying to pay off all the bills he hadn't quite figured on that were left over from Indianapolis. Threatening letters that make him panic. Finally, the phone company from Indianapolis gives him a way out—suggests sending a little money each month. He tries this with all his bills and relieves a little of the pressure.

Two months pass. Now Bruce has his car paid off. Now he can really get the bill collectors off his neck because he has collateral. There is only one problem. He is down again. And running short of day-to-day money.

"I try to give you enough," Penelope says.

"I know, I know," says Bruce. He gives his check to Penelope and she gives him an allowance. He tries to limit himself to a fifth of whiskey a day, but sometimes, particularly weekends, his control slips. Is it his control, or has the fatigue and the stress of the job caught up with him?

Does Bruce dare go downtown after he has called in sick? He must take some time sometime to negotiate a loan from his friendly loan company. Go ahead and take a chance. Bruce and Penelope talk to a helpful man who draws up the papers. It comes time for Bruce to sign his name. Bruce's hand is shaking very badly. He is a little nervous anyway, and he tried to stop drinking for a couple of hours before stopping in at the loan office.

Bruce excuses himself: "Have to visit the bathroom a

minute." Bruce sits down on the toilet and prays to God to make his hand stop shaking. Bruce is an atheist, but he is desperate. What do you do when the money is right there waiting to be picked up and you can't sign your name?

Bruce comes back out. The loan manager has mercifully moved to another desk to make a phone call. Bruce puts his left hand on his right hand and forces it through a series of chicken tracks that are vaguely identifiable as his signature, his mark, at least.

These days Bruce does have a supply problem. And sometimes in the middle of the day he will drive all the long way back to the apartment for five or ten minutes so he can have four or five quick drinks. He can't possibly afford the bar routine.

Penelope is still concerned but not devastated. Her pregnancy is proceeding beautifully. She and Bruce attend pre-birth classes at the Catholic hospital. Penelope suggests, "Why not try AA? Here's the phone number."

"Gee, I would," Bruce says, " but this town is so god-damned small, somebody would see me for sure and I'd be fired." Penelope understands.

Bruce has this feeling that he is on one end of a seesaw and that the whole wide world is piling up on the other end. There is no way he can get loose. He married Penelope a couple of years ago, at age thirty-two. She was the same age. No babes in the woods, but getting married was kind of an afterthought to "shacking up," as they called it in those days. "Shit or get off the pot," Penelope said. Bruce shit.

Bruce viewed his job as holding a scorpion by the tail. The debts and the pregnancy had him hemmed in, so he didn't dare look for a job elsewhere. He couldn't use his spare time as spare time. Because there wasn't any. Because he was either drinking or working or getting over drinking. And since getting over drinking meant work time lost, he would work some Saturdays and Sundays to make up for it. And get overtired by the next weekend so he drank too much again.

Most of all, the threat was the pregnancy. Bruce didn't want responsibility. Although Bruce loved children, he didn't want a lifetime of responsibility. So each day was almost overwhelming.

One Friday night Bruce comes home and Penelope says, "We never go anywhere."

"We can fix that," Bruce says, and after a few quick drinks he drives up into the mountains. This starts a Friday-night practice. Bruce and Penelope love the tall, brooding pines in the lengthening darkness, the touch of the cool mountain air.

"Don't you wish we had a house up here?" Bruce asks.

"Forever," says Penelope.

(Bruce thinks, A house in the high mountain meadow. Where the children play in the sunshine. Where the flickering firelight at night makes shadows dance against the wall.)

One Sunday morning Bruce and Penelope drive up into the mountains to an artificially created lake that has been stocked with trout. Bruce rents a pole and fishes. To make the afternoon go smoothly, he brings a jar of martinis. Does he catch a fish? Is he given a fish? There was a fish, he later remembers vaguely. The hours pass. It is late afternoon. Bruce stumbles to the car, too drunk to walk but ready to drive. Penelope follows.

Sunday afternoons the highways in and out of Resort City are jammed. On the way back home in a big, long line Bruce falls asleep while waiting for a traffic light to change.

Running

Two thousand horns toot. Penelope shakes and shakes Bruce
until he wakes up. Penelope is afraid Bruce will be arrested.
But the traffic is so jammed there isn't a policeman nearby.

Another month passes. Two of Bruce's and Penelope's
friends from Indianapolis are passing through, co-workers
from the television station. The group had been hard-
working and hard-drinking—this visit offers a chance to
celebrate.

A revelation comes to Bruce when he drinks with his
old-time friends. He begins to realize that he doesn't so much
have a drinking problem as a lack of friends to have fun with.
One friend back in Indianapolis had said, "If you find
yourself drinking alone, call me. I'll come over and drink with
you." Bruce wonders whether he still would be overdoing the
drinking if he had enough good friends around. "I work hard
and I play hard," says Bruce, repeating the slogan of many
business people and advertising people in particular. Bruce
knows he is more than ordinarily sensitive. And a very hard
worker. "A lot of people drink hard in this business," he says.

A few weeks later Bruce gets another clue that his
problems may be a little more complex than a simple ten-
dency to drink too much. His sister and brother-in-law come
driving through town and stop for a couple of days.

The first night Bruce's brother-in-law, Sam, says, "Let's
save a little money and have our cocktails at the apartment
before I take us out to dinner."

"Great," Bruce says. And while everyone is in the sitting
room, Sam says, "Your neighbors have excellent taste in
music." Bruce looks around and then realizes that Sam hears
Bruce's own radio, which is in the bookcase behind his chair.

"It's *my* radio," Bruce declares. Bruce suddenly realizes
that he has been judging himself too harshly. Here his

[59]

brother-in-law had made a silly little error in judgment. Everyone accepted it. If Bruce had done the same thing, there would have been an embarrassed silence. There would have been the implication that the drunk had done another dumb thing.

The next day everyone rides to the top of the mountain. Bruce throws snowballs at his nephew, and the nine-year-old kid doesn't quite know what is coming off at first. Possibly because Bruce is so bombed that nobody knows what he will be up to next. Upon coming down from the mountain and stopping in front of the apartment, Bruce leaps out and chases his nephew. And slips on the sand on the freshly tarred road. And falls heavily on his chest and shoulder.

Bruce is not a crybaby (and also doesn't want anyone to think he is falling-down drunk), so he gets up quickly and goes into the house and gets a drink. Later his sister sees the blood coming through his shirt. "Let me help," she says.

"It's nothing," Bruce says.

The next morning, Bruce shows his sister and brother-in-law and their children around the TV station. It is a Monday. As they turn to leave, Bruce's brother-in-law looks in his eyes. "Are you going to be all right?"

"I'll get by," he says.

Bruce works out a routine to swing his arm around so he can get both hands on the typewriter. Every key he types drives nails into his shoulder.

Later that day, Franklin yells in the doorway, "Important meeting tonight."

"Think I'll pass this one up," Bruce says.

"Better not. I honestly think you better not."

"Look, sweetheart," Bruce says, "my shoulder is killing me—I messed it up yesterday."

Running

"Honest, Bruce, you better come."

So Bruce not only works all day but into the evening. He wants to go across the street and get fortified, but he doesn't know exactly when Franklin is leaving and he has only a couple of bucks in his pocket. Finally it is time to climb into Franklin's powder-blue Cadillac and take the ride to a nearby city for dinner with the station owner.

At the restaurant Bruce orders a couple of beers, but drinking them is like pissing on the Chicago fire. There's horseplay about whether the owner will pick up the check for everybody. He does.

Strode, the owner, asks Bruce why he's having trouble keeping up with his work. Bruce says he has been assigned too many peripheral tasks in addition to the main duties of his job. Strode says Bruce is doing half as much as the previous person on the job. Bruce doesn't believe him but doesn't dare tell him he is full of shit. Bruce begins to get desperate.

That night Bruce's shoulder throbs so badly he can't sleep. The next few days he moves in a haze of pain. Even the booze isn't giving him much relief. Finally he gets an appointment with a doctor. It takes him about three hours' rotating in and out, getting X rays and all. It turns out he has a torn ligament. And the doctor says that since he has gone that long without a cast or sling he might as well tough it out the rest of the way to speed the healing process. So every night Bruce sweats deep in pain.

Two weeks after the dinner with the station owner, Bruce has managed to put together two weeks of consecutive work. Then another bad Monday comes along. He still goes in to work. And makes it through Tuesday, too. And Wednesday. Thursday is too much. And so is Friday. And Saturday he is so bombed that he doesn't lay in enough supply and Sunday he is out of booze.

"Let's drop in to see Franklin," Bruce says.

"What!" says Penelope.

"Drop in to see Franklin." Bruce figures Franklin might be serving drinks to people who drop in on a Sunday afternoon. It would be a swinging thing to do.

Penelope is horrified. "No, not after you've been home supposedly sick for three days."

"Well, let's go over and see Bill Gass then." They do.

Bill is watching a jungle animal rescue operation on TV. Bruce feels as if he is an intruder interrupting Bill's communion with the screen. And it turns out that Bill and his wife are about to go to someone's picnic. Bruce says he is just poking around trying to find something to do—that he is feeling very depressed.

"Depressed," Bill's wife, Shirley, says. "I've got it. Go to the zoo. Whenever I'm in the dumps, I go to the zoo."

"Yeah," Bruce says, "I guess that's a really great idea." He and Penelope leave for their zoo.

Bruce sweats and shakes the rest of the day. He sleeps a little that night and goes to work the next day. He lucks out and finds a parking place near the station. He sees traffic girl Jane walking thirty or forty feet ahead of him, her crow-black hair glistening in the sun, her seams straight. Bruce wants to whistle or call to her but she is a little too far away. The sun is bright. It is an absolutely beautiful morning.

Bruce climbs the stairs to his office and sees that somebody has really been working. Somebody has pulled out great stacks of material from his files. What a relief! It looks as if somebody said, "Let's give old Bruce a really big helping hand. Let's make this one time he comes back and he knows that somebody cared."

Bruce puts his fingers down on the space bar of his

typewriter and stutters it a little. Hell, he's not feeling half bad. Figures he might go down to the canteen and get a cup of coffee. Starts out the door of his office and there's Franklin. "Cup of coffee?" Bruce asks.

"Sure enough. I'll buy," says Franklin. They get their coffee out of the machine and Franklin starts talking last night's ball game to a couple of newsmen and Bruce sees Jane across the room. "Hi." No answer. "Hi, Janie." She turns and smiles and waves.

"Got something," Franklin says.

"Your place or mine," Bruce says.

"Yours."

They sit down in Bruce's office and Bruce's hands really aren't shaking noticeably—he hasn't spilled any coffee at all. Bruce shakes out a cigarette, lights it. "Who's the fairy godmother?" he asks, indicating the housecleaning.

"Jane and I," says Franklin. "Figured we'd get rid of some of this crap."

"Well, that's right neighborly," Bruce says.

"And this leads into what I have to tell you," Franklin says. "We got to talking over your situation and we came to the conclusion that you'd be better off out of here."

"Fired?"

"Well, you know, we work it so you get unemployment if you need it."

"Is there, uh, is there any alternative? This is kind of something I wasn't expecting."

"Look," Franklin says, "this job isn't right for you. We talked it over. I'll help you any way I can within reason—help you get another job in town if you want. But I think, if you're smart, you'll go back to Indiana where you have some friends and you can get things worked out for yourself."

[63]

"Would you like me to work out the day?"

"No, I have your check. You can just take off."

"Sure you don't want me to work out the day?"

"Sure."

"I wouldn't mind, uh, hanging around and taking these fucking files and setting a fucking match to them and really, uh, fucking up things."

"I know," Franklin says, "I *know.*"

Bruce has this feeling like he has been kicked in the stomach by a very big horse. He has had the breath knocked out of him. Bruce feels, This is not really me, this is not really real, he is handing me the check, I am taking the check, I am getting up, and it is now time for the alarm to go off and I will wake up and get ready to go to work.

And his ass aches. All around the rim. Not much point in driving uptown and fighting for a parking space near the bank. Walk up and cash the check before somebody changes his mind. Make plans.

Bruce hits the street. He is this broken-down cow-puncher going up Main Street for his last shootout. Only his crippled arm ain't no fucking good, Matt.

So this is the day that Bruce drives home with the empty cargo. Not forgetting to stop for a couple of jugs along the way.

What does Bruce do in the days ahead? He looks for advertisements for jobs in the newspaper. He doesn't call about them very often. He asks Penelope to call first. It means fewer times he has to try to untwist the cotton from around his anxious tongue.

He calls his friends. His friends don't know of any specific jobs, but they try to suggest other sources. Bruce believes his friends are worried. Friends are generally worried when they have friends in trouble, Bruce thinks. They wonder how much it is going to cost them.

Bruce calls Bill Gass. Bill tells him about a woman who wants an advertising salesman for her trade magazine. Bruce calls the woman and makes an appointment for lunch. (Now, take lunch. A lot of people have cocktails before lunch so if you smell a little booze before lunch you know that someone has been indulging in gracious living. That's all. In fact, don't you think people are getting a little nosy and judgmental if they think anything else?) So Bruce tosses off a few drinks over the morning, gearing himself to make a great impression and be hired for this fantastic job that pays something like $40 a week, which will never support him. In pouring rain he sets off for the restaurant in his car to capture this job and start his Big Comeback. In the heavy rain he can't find the restaurant, no matter how hard he tries.

Nothing turns up roses. Time is running out. After a few more days, Bruce calls Franklin and asks him if he can help locate a buyer for his car. Franklin says, "Sure, come on down." Bruce and Penelope call their relatives in an attempt to get enough money to go back to Indianapolis.

Selling his car is a surprise to Bruce. The used car dealer offers more than Bruce thinks it is worth. (But it's the exact amount needed to pay off the finance company loan.)

Penelope finds a giant-size wooden trunk at a junk shop on Main Street. Keep what will go into the trunk and suitcases. Sell everything else. Bruce and Penelope are shot down. Everything goes. Furniture. Dishes. Popcorn popper. Vacuum cleaner. Rugs. A neighbor lady will ship Penelope's iron to her. Sell all the baby stuff.

Last night. The TV station artist who lives just around

the corner gives them a farewell party their last night in Resort City. Their first time in his house. Of course, they had never invited him to their place, either. Various people from the station flow through. Mostly they don't speak to Bruce—mostly they have met him only once or twice. And they didn't know Penelope at all. Bruce and Penelope had made no attempt to know anybody—they were too busy. (And, Bruce thinks, Penelope has been too busy carrying MISS JESUS CHRIST in her belly. No time for people.)

To show that he is a man of taste, after inspecting the TV artist's work displayed on his walls, Bruce gives him a little advice. "You have a nice touch," he says, "but your inhibitions show. Why don't you let yourself go?"

The artist strokes his chin a second and then allows as to how Bruce can fuck himself.

After the artist's party that evening, Jane comes back to the apartment with Bruce and Penelope and volunteers to drive them to the airport the next morning. "But it's nearly two o'clock now and we leave at six," said Bruce. "We can get a cab."

"I want to do it," Jane says. So Bruce lets her. He knows that at bottom she is feeling guilty for conspiring against him. (It's always safer to remove a problem than to try and solve it. What about when Franklin and Jane had been deciding Bruce's future, why didn't they invite him into the discussion?)

Jane drives Bruce and Penelope to the airport. Bruce stands in line to pick up the tickets. He holds Shazzam, the cat, on his shoulder. Shazzam, terrified, digs his claws deep into Bruce's sore shoulder. Bruce needs a drink badly. He is starting to dry out again.

DANCERS
by Edward Gorman

Ass stomach (nice tummy) tits neck hair. Her hair feels blond. His fingers are very sensitive. But blond, she could be one of several. His fingers are not that sensitive.

He is checking her out blind because between his hangover and his exhaustion, he can't get his eyes open. And besides, he enjoys the game. Plays it often. Seeing if by touch alone he can remember whom he took home the previous night from this or that bar or party.

Then he withdraws his fingers, rolls over on his back again, and surrenders himself to his hangover. The worst of it is the dehydration. He once drank a six-pack of Pepsi in less than an hour. He paid for it later on the john, with bright hemorrhoidal blood.

In his head, his hangover is like a tumor. In his stomach, like a virus. Even his feet hurt, inexplicable.

The worst of his hangover wanes then, at least for the moment, and he starts to speculate again on the woman beside him.

He wonders if she is awake. He wonders if he knows her well enough (whoever she is) to fart. Really fart. He farts. Really farts.

He feels much better. As if some tense introduction has just been gotten through.

Next to him in the bed, she snores. Lightly. Peacefully.

Who could she be? There was the blonde who giggled and had buck teeth. There was the blonde who said that her main interest was art but kept mispronouncing Cézanne. There was the blonde who told him every ten minutes (and for no discernible reason) that she was originally from Los Angeles.

Probably she is one of them, this woman next to him.

And then he remembers a fourth blonde. The one who predicted that his son would end up on a shrink's couch clutching his balls. The one who told him that he was a piss-poor father and no better human being. The one who slapped him.

Now he can't recall how the episode started or finished. It seems he was just standing there, weaving slightly, talking to the blonde with the buck teeth, when for no reason this woman, who was actually nice-looking, made her way through the party and came right up to him. He recalls that her voice was hysterical and that for a long moment her otherwise lovely blue eyes were terrifying.

Then she slapped him. And after she slapped him, he left. Or she left. He can't remember which, and now it isn't important.

Now what matters is to open his eyes, the hell with the guessing game, the hell with his hangover, and see for sure who is lying next to him.

"Jesus Christ," he says.

Then, more roughly than he needs to, he begins shaking her shoulder. "Wake up."

As she struggles up through the fathoms of her sleep, he finds himself wishing she were bad-looking. A dog. A pig. Instead, she is a doe.

She even has a more than perfunctory smile for him. She asks, "What time is it?"

"Let's get one thing straight, lady. I see my son every chance I get."

Again she smiles. Her face is sensual with sleep. "I just asked the time."

"And I call him twice a week."

"I thought we settled this last night," she says.

"We didn't settle anything."

"We must've settled something," she says, "or what would I be doing here?"

He tries to glare at her. With the trouble he's having focusing, he probably just looks silly.

"Do you have a hangover?" she asks.

He says nothing and rolls to the other side of the bed, facing away from her.

His hangover is bad enough. And the day (whatever day it is) is ruined—in this condition, he'd have trouble jerking off, let alone doing anything constructive. And now her.

"Are you hungry?" she asks.

"No."

"Do you mind if I use your toothbrush?"

"Yes, I mind."

"Look," she says, moving closer to him. He can feel the heat of her all along the back of his body. "Look. We really did settle this. I apologized for saying what I did and for slapping you. Then we came over here and had a nice time. Don't you remember?"

He says nothing.

"Don't you remember?" she asks.

"Of course I remember."

"Well then?"

"Well then, nothing."

"I only said what I did because I was drunk. Because for some reason you reminded me of my ex-husband. But you're nothing alike. I told you that last night. When I apologized. You're nothing alike. He only sees our daughter once or twice a year. You see your son regularly."

"Not regularly."

"You said you did. Last night."

"Then I lied."

"Oh," she says. "Well, you see him sort of regularly."

"What the hell does that mean? 'Sort of' regularly?"

"More than once or twice a year."

"I don't see him as often as I could, and that's what matters. Not as often as I could."

"Well, you've talked to him then. On the phone."

"Not for three weeks."

"Oh," she says. "Then you've been busy and when you're not busy you'll start seeing him again. And phoning him again. Things come up from time to time. Women don't expect miracles."

He feels trapped now, hunched into a half-fetal, naked,

[70]

cold, lonely-as-a-monk position, unable to remember her name, let alone the crazy evening she's been describing in bits and pieces, guilty about his son and suffocatingly sorry for himself.

So she slapped him, he thinks. Well, maybe he had it coming. Maybe it was somehow his son slapping him.

"Women don't expect miracles," she repeats.

Now he rolls on his side the other way. Facing her. "Oh, really? Then what do women expect?"

She seems unimpressed by his hostility. "Women expect help."

He says, "He doesn't call her?"

"Sometimes when he's drunk. And then he cries and that just upsets her."

"Maybe he's got a reason to cry."

"Of course he does. We all do. But he should think of our daughter before he thinks of himself."

He doesn't know how to deal with her. If she'd remained the woman who shrieked at him, who slapped him, maybe now they could have some mean sex and then he could kick her out. But she's not that simple.

"You want some breakfast?" he asks.

"If you'll let me use the bathroom."

"There's a new toothbrush in the medicine cabinet. I'll start breakfast."

He lets her get up first. With his hangover, he will dodder like an old man and he looks old enough these days.

But she doesn't go into the bathroom immediately. She stands naked at the foot of the bed looking down at him, combing through her blond hair with her fingers. He guesses her age at thirty. She has small breasts and tender-looking thighs. And light freckles across her nose. About freckles he can get sentimental. He doesn't like women he can't get sentimental about.

"I really am sorry about last night," she says.

"I've done things like that myself. I'm a bad drunk."

He expects her to deny this. To say that she's the bad drunk, not he.

She says nothing.

"As a matter of fact, I can be a very nasty drunk."

"I'll be right back," she says and gives him a tricky, nervous smile and starts off for the john.

He decides against dressing, not even underwear, though his stomach after thirty-six years is not exactly flat and his body is not exactly tanned. His first steps are painful. The tumor in his head expands. This morning he could drink a case of Pepsi, not just a six-pack.

As he moves toward the little kitchenette concealed behind the latticework doors, he wonders again why she was silent when he said he was a nasty drunk. Then his stomach tightens. It occurs to him that he has no real recollection of the previous night. For a moment he is terrified, thinking of all the things he might have said or done. But if he'd gone off, really fucked it up, why would she be here?

He opens the latticework doors.

The stove top is gummy with the grease of three thousand eggs and ten thousand strips of bacon, but not half as gummy as the pan into which he puts the fresh eggs and bacon. His coffeepot burned out long ago, so he now boils water for instant coffee in a battered little pan. He can hear her pissing and then flushing the toilet. He puts two plates and some reasonably clean silver on the table. He hears her running water in the sink and then gargling. He sets two slices of bread in the toaster. He hears her closing the medicine cabinet and opening the bathroom door.

He turns to watch her walk toward him. He is still wondering why she wouldn't deny that he's a terrible drunk. He looks at her face carefully. She looks happy enough.

"You need any help?" she asks.

"It's all ready," he says, coming away from the kitchenette with a sticky jug of orange juice in his hand.

"Not bad," she says after taking the first bite of her omelet.

"Not good, though."

She laughs. "Not bad."

"So how did we finally get together?" he asks after he finishes his first cup of coffee.

She looks disappointed. "You don't remember any of it, do you?"

"Some of it. Not all of it."

"None of it. It's not worth talking about anyway," she says.

"I'm just curious."

"There's nothing to be curious about."

"Well, why did you slap me?"

"Because I was drunk."

"How did we get from there to here?"

"You don't remember any of it, do you?"

He sighs. "Not much."

"Not any."

Now she sighs. "All right. All right, but then we drop the subject, okay?"

"Okay."

"After I slapped you, I left the party and went downstairs. I was so upset I couldn't even start my car. I just sat there crying. The more sober I got, the more embarrassed I got. Then I noticed you sort of weaving your way to your car. I decided to apologize. Which is what I tried to do. But you wouldn't let me."

The tumor is working on the front part of his brain now. He wants to tell her to stop. Why upset her more by making her go through it all again? Why risk upsetting himself by hearing about something he did or said while drunk? "You mean I wouldn't accept your apology?"

She smiles. "You didn't think I owed you an apology. You said that you didn't know who I was. At first I thought you were just being belligerent. How could you forget somebody who'd just slapped you ten minutes ago? But then I realized how drunk you were. You honestly didn't know who I was."

He tries for a smile. "Sometimes I drink too much."

"So I told you all about it. About what I'd said to you, how you were a terrible father and a selfish person. And about how I'd slapped you."

"Did I get hostile?" he asks.

"You tried to lay me."

"Right there in the parking lot?"

"Right on the car hood."

"That isn't funny. I apologize."

"At least I persuaded you to get inside the car."

"We did it inside the car?"

"In the front seat. Just like high school. It was sad. But I thought it would settle our debt."

"So how did we get to my place?" he asks.

"I drove us. Your car is still in the parking lot."

"Christ," he says. He remembers none of what she's

describing. None of it. He is terrified. "Could we get back into bed?"

"Into bed?" She looks surprised. "Why?"

"Why do you think?"

As a boy he played a certain game. He imagined that his bed was a life raft and that as long as he stayed in bed nothing could harm him. Not the sharks. Not the ocean. Now, as he makes love to her, he feels this same peace and security again. He watches her face. She looks at peace, too. And now he no longer worries about last night, or even about his hangover.

"Thank you," he says afterward.

For a while then he is silent, here on his life raft, surrounded by sharks and the cold eternal ocean.

But he knows his contentment is not permanent. He still has questions. What else he said. What else he did. He has to know. His raft is a bed again.

He says, "I'd like to apologize for last night."

"We're not going to talk about last night anymore, remember?"

"But I do owe you an apology."

"For what?" she asks. "I was the one who slapped you."

"But after that," he says. "For the parking lot. For that I owe you an apology. For that I apologize."

"Well," she says. "For the parking lot I guess I would accept an apology. A small one."

"A big one. I know what I'm like when I'm that drunk."

"A small one will be fine," she says.

"Is there anything else I should apologize for? About last night?"

"Please. Forget about last night," she says.

[75]

"Did I talk about my son?"

"Please."

"Well, did I?"

"You said he was very bright and very kind and that you loved him very much."

"Did I talk about visiting him?"

"You said you visited him regularly."

"Well, I don't. That was an exaggeration. I don't visit him regularly."

She says nothing.

He says, "I don't want you to think I'm like your ex-husband."

"He's not so bad," she says. "Not really. It's just when he hurts Jennifer. But after being with you, I understand him a little better."

"Me? What did I have to do with it?"

"Why the hell do you keep pushing?"

"I want you to tell me. You're holding something back and I want you to tell me what it is."

"Please. I have to leave in an hour. I don't want to waste it talking about last night."

"You can always leave now."

"Maybe I will," she says.

"But before you go, I want you to tell me about last night."

"What you did is nothing to be ashamed of."

"I'll be the judge of that."

"Can't we just lie here?"

"What did I do?"

She says, "You tried to call your son."

"What?"

"You tried to call your son. It was three-thirty in the morning. I wouldn't let you. We wrestled by the phone over there."

"Jesus," he says.

She says nothing.

He says, "Why the hell did I try to call my son at three-thirty in the morning?"

"Because you felt sorry for yourself."

"For him."

"For yourself."

"Jesus Christ," he says.

"It's nothing to be ashamed of. All of us have reasons to feel sorry for ourselves."

"Jesus," he says.

She tries to put her arms around him. He leans back to make this impossible. Now he is sick of her, of himself. His hangover threatens to push his eyes out of his head.

"I suppose you feel really smug about all this," he says after a while.

"Hardly."

"You know I could make a point right here."

"If it will make you feel better," she says, "make it."

"I could ask you where your daughter is at this very moment. And where she's been all night."

"At home. With my mother."

"With your mother. You don't think your daughter misses you when you're gone?"

"Of course she does."

"But even knowing that she misses you, you go out anyway? And stay out all night?"

"Yes."

"Well what kind of mother does that make you? Your daughter's at home missing you and here you are in some man's bed. What kind of mother does that make you?"

"I only go out one night a month," she says.

"Very noble."

"One night a month," she says. "One night a month I have my mother watch Jennifer so I can stay out all night. So I can get laid, screwed, fucked, whatever you want to say. I don't have a steady boyfriend. This is the only thing I can do and I make no apologies for it. No fucking apologies whatsoever. Do you understand?"

He says nothing. What can he say? Then he says, "I'm sorry."

She says nothing.

He says, "I'm sorry."

"Of course you're sorry," she says. "Of course you're sorry. And I'm sorry. And Jennifer's sorry. And my ex-husband's sorry. We're all sorry."

"Your one night a month," he says. "You could've found somebody better to spend it with than me."

"Or somebody worse," she says. "There are lots worse."

"Not 'lots' worse," he says.

"All right," she sighs. "Not 'lots' worse."

HOUSEWIFE

by Wilbur Cross

Is there any reward in being a housewife, especially with three small children, a large, muddy-footed dog, a budget an Eskimo couldn't live on in the Far North, and a husband who is seldom home and has a girlfriend on the side?

Is it fun and games to watch food hardening on plates which then have to be scraped and washed by hand because the dishwasher has been broken for more months than you can remember? Is it like taking a holiday trip to trudge down four flights of stairs in a dimly lit apartment building to the basement laundry room and stick quarters in noisy machines that leak all over your feet?

Yes. Yes. Yes. I found the magic formula that brought instant appeal to those dreaded household chores.

I had just gotten my period, which makes me mean and sickish at best. My dear husband had phoned the night before from Detroit, where he was on a business trip, to say that his business had been "extended." The children had all been late getting off to school. The dog had thrown up in the living room. And I was making my second trip to the catacombs with two pillowcases stuffed with foul-smelling dirty laundry.

Yet I could hardly wait to get down the echoing metal stairs, which I hated with enormous fury as a symbol of what my life had become—hollow, cold, hard, ugly, metallic. Down there, in the menial mine shaft, I had an uncommon reward, one I had "discovered" just two days earlier with the inadvertent help of a neighbor down the hall.

"Don't you take a can of beer down with you?" she had asked when I met her coming up from the laundry room. "I always take my brew—one can for each load. It helps pass the time. And I deserve some goodie for dragging myself down into the bowels two or three times a week."

A "goodie." That was the answer. The only thing was, I detested beer. I decided to make a Bloody Mary. I would take it down and set it on the shelf where the detergent was kept, and I would drink it while I was reading the paperback novel I always took down with me. If I had to wash two loads of laundry, I would take *two* Bloody Marys. My neighbor had the right idea. One goodie per load.

I had never made a Bloody before, but I had seen my husband do it. I filled about a third of a glass with vodka. Then tomato juice. And about a spoonful of steak sauce (we didn't have any of that Wooster stuff). And some pepper and salt and a piece of parsley for looks.

By the time I finished my first Bloody and the first load of laundry was tumbling out of the dryer, I knew that Life Can Be Beautiful, even in the basement of Hillcrest 22A. The clothes were hot and clean and soft to the touch. I scooped them up and pressed a big armful to my breast.

Already I was thinking that maybe I should go right upstairs and get a second load. The towels needed washing, and that little rug in the back hall where the kids had spilled orange drink. I'd bring down a second Bloody Mary.

By the time I had finished the second load and the second drink, it was a little after noon and time for lunch. I made myself a tuna fish sandwich. I also made a third Bloody Mary to celebrate my liberation from drudgery. I thumbed through an old copy of *Ladies' Home Journal* and laughed over the ads. There was one telling how life would be so much more enjoyable for housewives who cooked with that magic ingredient, rice. Another described a detergent with formula X or Z, included by the public-spirited manufacturer to make washing clothes a "joy." A third touted a new brand of cigarette as the way to make life sparkle.

Hah, hah, hah. I laughed loudly and uproariously so that the sound echoed through the kitchen and bounced off the ceiling. There is only one magic ingredient on earth and *I have found it.* Liquor!

For the next couple of months, I lived happily in my newfound world, with my own Blue Bird of Happiness at my side. When it was apparent what wonders a drink could do for washing clothes, I applied the same solution to scrubbing the bathroom, cleaning the oven, or changing the sheets. I experimented with other kinds of drinks that could be concocted from vodka, rye, or rum, the only three liquors my husband kept in the closet. A daiquiri in the bathroom, vodka and tonics while working the bedrooms. A stiff whiskey sour when facing the challenge of a grease-encrusted oven.

It never struck me that I was opening the door to problem drinking. In fact, I was in a state of ecstasy over having *closed* the door on my problems and entered a new world of living, not just existing. The only real problem that came up was one of supply and demand.

"Where in hell is the vodka bottle?" I could hear my husband shouting from the kitchen on one of the evenings when he did come home. "It's gone. You never drink vodka. Did someone borrow it?"

"Oh, I meant to tell you," I purred innocently, an excuse springing to my lips as easily as if I had rehearsed it all afternoon. "I was getting out some cans of spaghetti (I recalled instantly that they were on the same shelf) and I knocked down the bottle and it smashed."

From then on I was careful to have a dual supply—I referred to it as "His and Hers" in my bemused merriment. At this stage of my progression, it was very simple to set aside part of the food and clothing budgets, miserly though they were, for booze. I was buying mostly pints and stashing them away behind the sugar and flour and other staples that he would never touch.

When my demand reached a point where it was getting tough to juggle the budget this way, I had my first twinge of guilt. Maybe I was slopping away too much of the hard stuff. "Take it easy, Emily girl," I said to myself. But then I thought, You're no drunk. You have a nip only as a reward. And if you perform more chores, you deserve more rewards. That's not the drinking pattern you see in someone who's a lush.

What I overlooked, whether deliberately or not, I don't know, was the fact that the *one* cocktail I drank as a goodie, a reward, was now at least double the strength of the cocktail I had fashioned for the same purpose five or six months ago. Also—and I did not realize this until much, much later—I was very cleverly deceiving myself in a related way: When I had an ordinary load of laundry to take to the basement ("game room," as I now called the laundry room), I would carefully sort it into two piles. The kids' clothes haven't been coming out as white and bright as they should be, I would rationalize. Surely I must be cramming too many clothes into the machine at one time. This way, I earned *two* drinks, instead of just one.

It was tough fooling myself the evening they found me in the laundry room, passed out cold. I don't remember what happened, but I can piece together the whole messy tale this way: I had overslept that morning, and when I pried myself out of bed the children had already left for school. One of them had left me a note. My husband was out of town, as usual. Nothing much mattered except the fact that my head was in a vise and my hands were shaking so badly I had to put the note down on the table before I could read the childish scrawl. I had to have a drink—as medicine, something to calm my nerves. It was really the first time I had resorted to drinking before breakfast. But the mixture of cold orange juice heavily laced with vodka worked like a miracle drug. Within ten minutes I was in complete command of myself, ready for the day. I would not have any drinks that day, I told myself, or do any housework, other than a little bit of straightening up. Then I'd go to the market and buy a roast, a steak, something extravagant (after all, if I was not going to have any drinks I'd really be saving several dollars, so the meat would be a bonus). My husband was coming back from his trip and I'd make up to the children for not having cooked them any breakfast.

That was about ten-thirty. By noon, the headache was coming back again and I felt edgy. No way to be, if we were all going to have a nice family dinner and play Togetherness. Out came the vodka bottle that I had carefully hidden behind the sugar sack. Out came a bottle of tomato juice. Two drinks later, everything was rosy again—except for one small annoyance. I had let a half-filled bottle of tomato juice slip through my fingers and the braided rug in the kitchen was a bloody mess. No harm. No harm. Down you go to the laundry room, where everything is magically transformed. Including Emily, that former pumpkin who has been turned into a Princess.

Down we go. Everything to be salubrious. (Is that really a word?) The Greatest. Oops. We have our little drink with us. But we forgot the rug, all saturated with liquid red vitamins. Fortified. Hah! What time? About three-thirty.

The last thing I remember was looking at my watch and going upstairs to pour another drink. The rug had completed its cycle and had come out of the machine looking almost as dirty as when I had stuffed it in and spun the dial. Which was not odd because I had forgotten to add any detergent.

As the hours went by, the children returned from school, at first surprised, then increasingly worried when they were unable to find out where I was or when I intended to return. My husband came through the apartment door, overnight bag in hand, about seven-thirty, to find three frightened, teary children. He was ready to call the hospital and the police about two hours later, when a neighbor knocked frantically on the door to say that she had found me. I was lying on a pile of laundry in the basement.

"Maybe it's a stroke," she said in a voice that sent the children into hysterics, "or she fell and bumped her head and got knocked out."

I was knocked out all right. Soused. Zonked. Bombed.

My husband, who is large and strong, carried me upstairs like a bag of wet cement and threw me on the bed and slammed the door shut, leaving the children whimpering outside and wondering in uncontrollable sobs how soon Mommy was going to die.

Unfortunately, Mommy did not die. She was just entering a long, chaotic era of drinking which was not to end until she had been committed five times to state mental institutions and confined for long periods in the most depressing kind of drying-out wards. I remember those days as a series of intense nightmares, made all the more acute because of the interim periods when I was permitted to go free.

Incarceration, threats, tragedies, critical illness, physical and mental torture—none of these gruesome expediencies makes much impression on the alcoholic mind. It is like trying to write a message on ice with a crayon.

What finally kept my hand off the cork?

I'll tell you what. At the age of thirty-seven (give or take a few years—I can't really remember too clearly), I looked seventy, acted ninety. I was too completely exhausted to drink any longer, let alone work or play. My husband had left me. My children were taken away from me. I was existing on welfare and a pitifully small allowance—I didn't get alimony, I was so far beyond mounting any legal action on my behalf.

I contemplated suicide, but was too goddamned debilitated to wreak any physical violence on my person, and too poverty-stricken to hoard a supply of pills.

So I joined AA. More correctly, I was taken by the hand and led every night, and sometimes during the day, to meeting after meeting.

I stopped drinking. But AA is hardly a social club. I don't make friends there. Don't learn much about how to go out in the real world and make my way. Don't get religion, or promises that the future will be rosy.

"Work the program," says the fat, wide-faced hairdresser who is my sponsor, "work the program, dearie. And come to meetings. And don't drink—one day at a time."

And I think I'll throw up on the floor if anyone tells me this "one-day-at-a-time" crap anymore. But I listen to that sh— crap. And maybe it gets to you sometimes. The other evening at a closed meeting there was this guy who was a clown. And I mean it, he had been a clown at a circus until the booze got him kicked out on his ass. And he was really funny, telling about the time he was drunk on stilts. And I startled the whole group by laughing like I had suddenly popped a firecracker in my teeth.

I hadn't done that for a long, long time. Maybe three years.

There could be some hope, yet.

A QUICKIE
by Richard F. Radford, Jr.

The strollers and joggers on the banks of the expressway weren't paying particular attention to the traffic pattern below. But if they were, the frustrated lane-shifting of the battered, neglected, once-aqua '64 Chevy would have made it obvious to them that its driver was in a hurry.

Inside the car, except for his left arm, which was wildly and angrily gesticulating out the window, was James Smith, thirty years old, American, male, husband, and soon-to-be father of his second child.

Jimmy had a problem. A problem he couldn't define. Like knights of old defending a castle, Jimmy felt besieged. The only difference was, those old knights *knew* who the enemy was, they could be pinpointed and identified as they arrayed in battle formation out in the open. The "things" that beset Jim were sneaky, ill-defined, and nameless. He could never just grab one and say, "Here, this is what's been bothering me!" He could never get a handle on "them." "They" were just *there.*

Although the only "real" living Jimmy did these days was in his imagination, there was nothing imaginary about the angry heat he could feel rising from his neck, along the sides of his face, and coming to a simmering halt in the middle of his forehead just above his eyes. Jim needed a drink.

"Christ," began the dialogue with himself, an ongoing dialogue that never quite ceased—even when he was talking with, or listening to, someone.

"I've got to get to Lynch's early enough for a *couple*—just to cool down. . . . Jeez, if I'm not home in time tonight, Ann'll kill me, even though I was pretty good at the party last night. For a change. . . . Just two fast ones to stop this pounding and smooth the edges of my nerves. Tough day today. I *deserve* one—or two!"

He chuckled, knowing he had never had just one in his life. Furthermore, he didn't trust those limp-wrists who did come into Lynch's each night, had One, then left!

"There must be something in their past, something they're ashamed of and are afraid of blurting out if they loosen up," he thought. "Too uptight to drink like *men*—they probably don't ever wear the pants at home—"

"Dammit! Is this old bag in front of me dragging her foot, or does she have an anchor trailing from the bumper?" He pounded on the horn and jerked the wheel to pass her on the right.

The screeching protest of his bald front tires reminded him to take fewer chances. He hadn't gotten around to fixing the flat spare in the trunk. He'd meant to do that after he taped the leaky radiator hose. "Too many demands on my time. . . . There just isn't enough time. . . . Where does it all go?

A Quickie

... Ahh ... two more blocks to Lynch's." His nerves seemed to calm just at the thought.

The patrons of Denny Lynch's Bar & Grille–Ladies Invited—who were regularly ensconced on stools with a view out the large plate-glass window—were adept at predicting who would be the next customer through the door.

As Jimmy's faded old Chevy shuddered illegally to a stop at the hydrant in front, these regulars visibly brightened. Someone shouted, "Heeeere's Jimmy!"

Delight and expectation could be read on the faces of all in the bar who were "in the know" because, after all, wasn't Jimmy quick to buy a round and tell a funny story or return a borrowed sawbuck. "God," they said, "doesn't Jimmy love a good time!" "Can he drink!" "I've never seen him with a package on."

Jimmy approached the door through the bright sunshine. Of average height and stocky build, what made Jim the type you'd bring home to Mom was the cherubic weak-featured face that exuded boyish charm. Round face, heavily freckled chubby cheeks, and thinning light brown, almost blond hair. Though his teeth were as neglected as his car, people didn't notice because his smile was so engaging despite what might be called "thin" lips. But what was outstanding about Jim's looks were his watery blue eyes. Eyes that even when wrinkled in smiling made the observer think the owner knew pain. Haunting eyes that hinted at unspoken sadness. Mystical eyes.

In a flash, conscious and unconscious, Jimmy took in the mood, the feel of the entire place before he had stepped three paces inside the door. It was a sixth sense he had that worked whenever he went anywhere. Another facet of his supersensitivity.

Coming off the ramp of the expressway Jimmy had planned to sit at the front end of the bar tonight because tonight he was *definitely* having only two and then straight home to Ann. Ann was really touchy these days—"but chalk it up to the impending arrival. Things will be better after the baby comes and things get back to normal."

Seeing that the front end of the bar was filled with regulars and a few standing itinerants, Jim proceeded without a hitch, except for a few fraternal backslaps and offhand joking insults, to his accustomed, unoccupied throne at the rear end of the bar. From this vantage point Jim could view all who entered his temporary fiefdom as well as tune in on any conversation, at any point; plus watch the bartender to make sure he made Jim's highball dark brown—the way he liked it.

"Might as well get your money's worth," he mused. "Besides spending my own, I keep the others in here. Should throw a guy one for nothing once in a while, let 'im know they appreciate him."

Jim's highball with the usual beer chaser, or Abbott and Costello, as he called it, were waiting at their rendezvous before he got there, because the bartender knew from past experience that Jim got very testy while waiting. His remarks would be couched in jocular tones, but there was a barely hidden cutting edge to them—like a rock in a snowball—that cut deep when they landed.

Basking in the attention he received, Jim's spirits lifted (punning to himself, he lifted the spirits in the glass) and he *swore* he felt better physically, too, just walking into Lynch's. "Keyed-up executives *must* unwind," he said to himself, as he noticed Jack at the opposite end of the long bar signal to the bartender for a refill for himself and Jim. "Funny how my senses are so radar-sharp and I notice those things." Without yet acknowledging to Jack that he had caught the signal (he would feign surprise when the drink arrived), Jim sort of half burped through his nose the beer that was going down his throat as though it had jagged edges.

Unaware that he was comforted by the thought of the second drink coming while the first was only half finished, Jim *was* glad he was saving a dollar because tonight he was having only two, then scramming.

The running conversation he held with all and sundry (democratically including the "losers" who were part of every bar scene) was but secondary to what went on inside his head.

The second drink slid silkily down.

"I don't know what Ann sees wrong in me stopping for a few. Feels good to relax after a day lifting planks on that construction job. Damn foreign foreman, always picking on *me*. Doesn't he see the others goofin' off? Why me? Job sucks. But she's got no complaint, I bring home the check, don't I? She always bitched about my sales jobs, never knowing how much I'd bring home. This is less money, but *she* likes it, cuz she can count on it. *I* don't like it. If they hadn't cut my territory, I'd still be in a suit and tie. Sales is tough. A guy works his butt off building up a territory—then *they* cut it up. I showed them. James Paul Smith, Jr., wouldn't stand for that. I got out. Good timing, too. They'll probably fold. Sales Manager Quits. How did that look to the home office? Can't they see? Got out of there just in time, too, before the glory-boys with their college diplomas took over. Wouldn't know a real salesman if they fell over him. Never finished my education. Could've though. Bunch of rinky-dinks. Studying. Didn't know what *real* life was all about. Got my education where it counts. Intelligence, not erudition. I've got common sense, experience, and I know *people*. That's where it's at. Next time I'll pick a small company, one that's growing and will appreciate what I've got to offer. That's if they can see beyond the sheepskin to give me a chance. Next time will be different. Oh, oh. Jack's looking at me, I'd better reciprocate or he'll think I'm a cheapskate."

"Bartender! Ale for my men, water for my horses, and serve ye well my vassal John!"

"I've got time for one more quickie. Ann won't have dinner ready yet. Ann. She can't gripe about the party last night. We were only a little late getting there and I behaved like a gentleman. Didn't insult one of her dumb friends— even fat dumb Alice and her insipid husband, 'Successful Sam.' God! If he had mentioned one more time that he was vice-president of that stupid company, I'd have decked him. Lucky bastard. If he hadn't married the boss's dumb ugly daughter, he'd be in the unemployment line. He couldn't even lug planks like me. Where does she find these idiot friends? Smug in their suburbs and P.T.A. crap, they don't know what *real* life is all about. Bet none of them had to scramble for a buck as a kid, or ever went hungry, for that matter. My old man was a drunk, but who wouldn't be, married to that witch. Christ, what fights! Poor unlucky slob, life treated him like dirt. I loved 'im. Even if he was legless, he'd come up smilin'. I'd never be like him, though. Even if I do drink a lot, I always eat. Gotta protect the liver. Plus, I always know what I'm doin'. I always drive home, don't I? Drove home last night, too. Clever. Closed the left eye so she couldn't see. Lousy watery drinks at that party, gotta drink two for one just to stay even. Better than that skinflint Pat, he gives you one, then lets you rattle ice cubes all night. Just cuz he doesn't drink. Don't trust him."

The change from the last round lying on the bar persuaded Jim there was time for one last fast one before he left.

"Umm, at least this one tastes like there's something in it."

Glancing in the bar mirror to his right for the umpteenth time, Jimmy decided he liked his profile. The set of his chin looked ultra-masculine, even if he did need a haircut.

'The one-drink fags are coming and going like waves on the shore. Here for a second and gone. Wife's probably at the front door with a stopwatch and breathalizer. What the hell's the sense of having just one? Can't drink like a man, might as well not stop in. Join the Holy Rollers or something. Hey! There's Sully and Ed just come in. Good guys. I owe them a drink."

"Bartender, give Sully and Ed, my old pals, a pop. No, none for me, I'm goin'. . . . Well, okay, one for the road, a bird can't fly on one wing."

"If I'm a few minutes late, she'll have to grin and bear it. After all, it's not like I'm late *every* night. Cripes, some of these guys never go home and their wives have to work, too. Not her, she's got it pretty good. She knew what I was like before she married me. A few good belts loosen me up, bring out the best in me. If I ever write the Great American Novel, these characters from Lynch's will be in it. F. Scott Fitzgerald was a drinker; Poe, too. Got their inspiration from a bottle. Seems I have my best, deepest thoughts when I've got just a slight buzz on. Have to write 'em down one of these days. If I can ever get everybody off my back long enough."

Sully and Ed had bought a round back. Now Jim's change was too large for a tip, but just right for one drink and a tip—as if there were something unmanly about removing money from the bar once displayed there.

"A fast dash, barkeep. I've miles to go before I sleep." To prove he meant it this time, Jim gulped his drink greedily, shaking his head over the protests at his leaving while signaling to the bartender that the change was his, and strode briskly out the door.

"There!" he announced to the Chevy in the darkness. Satisfied, he settled behind the wheel and turned the key, applauding his good fortune at the lack of a ticket on the windshield.

"Congratulations, Jim, my boy, you've proved you can stop for just a few. Supper will kill the little glow and you can have a couple of sociables with Ann afterwards and she'll be happy. Who says you can't handle it? Christ, a man's got to have *something*, doesn't he? Tonight will prove things are going to be different. After the baby comes, I'll get a better job and throw a real bash. That'll show her folks. Come to think of it, if I only drank at home, she couldn't complain about *anything*. The money we'd save could go toward that TV she's been hinting at. Plus, she couldn't complain that I'm never home. If she'd keep that crummy apartment neater, I'd be home more. Sure I explode. Who wouldn't with all I've got to contend with? Fickle fate has certainly not been in *my* corner. Bills, Jeez. Am I the only one who owes Sears & Roebuck?

"If everybody'd stay off my back a few minutes I could think this out. Straighten the whole mess out when I get on my feet. Thank God I *am* a drinker, at least I get some relief. No wonder those other guys have heart attacks and nervous breakdowns. All work and no play . . . Can only bend so far, then you snap. Gotta have some escape. Thesis: Demands of Society on Modern Male.

"There's the Corner Pub. No. Not tonight, gotta get home. Things'll get better. The 'boys' won't die on the vine if they don't see me tonight. Hmmm. Eight-thirty. I'll bet they're really whoopin' it up after the ball game. Lucky stiffs.

A Quickie

No ties on their time. Do what they want. Damn car wants to
stop. Jeez, I do have to use the john, didn't go at Lynch's,
such a goddamn hurry to screw home. Maybe I'll go to the
john and have just one to catch the score. Just a quickie."

YOU CAN KEEP
THE FOX

by S. A. Robbins

He looked like George Washington on the dollar bill
that had been forgotten in a pants pocket and laundered with
the rest of the wash: empty, wrinkled, and bleached. As he
ordered breakfast, consisting of the celery stalk in his "Not-
So-Bloody" Mary, he gave me his ritual rationale for a
morning hangover and subsequent afternoon intoxication.

"Dog of the hair that bites you," he whispered, pulling a
celery string from his teeth.

J. B. Pitts was the president of his family business,
occasionally taking important phone calls at the bar but more
often than not asking me to take a message while he was in
conference with a bottle of Ballantine. In reality, he was only
a glorified janitor and his company was merely a crew of
maids and garbage men, but he lived his life in grand style,
complete with silver-knobbed canes and three-piece suits
imported from England. As his wife confided one evening

before she carried him home, "J. B. Pitts never does the dirty work himself."

"There's a hole in the bottom of my glass, Barcheap!" he bellowed from the end of the bar that he called his office. This was J.B.'s way of asking for a refill.

Unlike other customers, who enjoy a clean glass with each new order, J. B. Pitts demanded each drink in the same glass, so that at the end of "office hours" he could determine how much he owed by the number of lemon-peel twists in the bottom of the glass.

"Just check the lemon if you don't believe me," he would always scold as he left the bar. His record was twenty-seven. "If only them lemons could talk . . ." was another of his favorite sayings.

In point of fact, J. B. Pitts was a man of clichés. When he couldn't recall the appropriate aphorism, he would fall into a meditative silence in search of the words, then blurt them out too late in the conversation to have any meaning, which led most casual observers to conclude that this Janitor Extraordinaire was going mad.

"Another hole in my glass! I demand to see the manager of this establishment," he repeated theatrically. I refilled his glass, adding today's fifth lemon twist, and awaited his next predictable utterance.

"Not so much water this time, Barcheap, there's a drought in this state . . . or don't you read the papers?" I gave him the Ballantine and water, which made him repeat the question, loudly enough so that everyone could hear. Only then was I allowed to respond.

"No, J.B., I don't read the papers." This set J.B. up for another of his favorites.

"Another egghead bites the dust. . . . The yolk's on you,

Humpty Bumpty." At this he laughed uproariously, as if he had coined the boring pun himself. That was my cue to laugh with him. And so we performed our daily di-monologue, for whoever was within range of the booming rasp that was J.B.'s voice.

Occupying the only other seat in the area known as J.B.'s office was the silent Murphy Malone, an ex-boxer turned weekend bandleader, who could drink manhattans all day and all night. Often he did just that. Wearing an old luminescent green tuxedo, the red-faced Murphy Malone looked like last year's Christmas greetings. Murphy ordered another manhattan by tapping his glass with a swizzle stick, and J. B. Pitts exclaimed, "You're full of baloney, Maloney."

Pitts laughed, but Malone was sad as usual and remained silent.

"What's the matter, Mad Hatter? Cat got your phony Irish tongue?" Pitts nudged Malone in the ribs with his walking stick, and Malone belched the belch of a true Man of Drink.

"Well put, Irish orchestra boob. I couldn't have said it better with my own two ruby lips. . . . Barcheap, my glass is empty again. I thought I asked you to plug that hole. Well, plug it again, Sam!" I filled his drink as requested, plopped another lemon peel in among the rest, and retreated to my inventory sheet, which I used as an excuse when I lacked the energy to participate in the strange one-sided conversation between the two regulars.

As he always did after his seventh highball, J. B. Pitts began telling the same bad jokes in an effort to draw Malone out of his shell. He was in the middle of the one about the two ethnic persons and a monkey wrench when the usually silent Murphy Malone, for reasons unknown at the time, began to sob. Pitts ignored the tears until he delivered the punch line, then requested another round in classic fashion.

"Quick, Barcheap, the sponge! And you can hold the water in the next round—Maloney here is my faucet."

I poured the two confederates another round and tossed another lemon peel into the glass with the proverbial hole. Murphy's mysterious tears ended as abruptly as they had begun, and still without an explanation. Murphy served as J.B.'s silent partner, and Pitts tolerated him for that reason: the less Malone said, the greater opportunity for Pitts to talk. And talk.

Pitts had reached the point in describing his two St. Bernards when he normally produced pictures of the dogs, when Malone broke his code of silence and began to complain about his father, an aged invalid who lived in the spare room of Malone's condominium. What followed was a dual monologue, both Malone and Pitts talking concurrently. (The inevitable chronological progression of words in print undermines any attempt to reproduce this duet honestly, and I am forced to relate this concurrent oratory as dialogue, which it was not.)

(Malone)

"The old fart was unhappy his whole life and is determined that mine will be just the same: nothing. My entire income is invested in hospital bills, oxygen tanks, private nurses, and do you think he appreciates any of this? Hell no; he says I owe it to him. I owe it to *him*. As if it was my fault he's dying of leukemia, as if it was *my* fault he has a double hernia, as if it was *my* fault . . ."

(Pitts)

"Bozo and Lady are smart as people, I tell you, smarter

than my stupid wife for sure. *They* tell *her* when it's time to eat, time to sleep, time to go for a walk. And believe you me, when those dogs want to walk, they walk. Or else. And you know what 'or else' means, don't you Maloney? Up to your tootsies in dog crap. There was this time me and the Missus were away for the weekend and you shoulda seen . . . "

(Malone)

". . . that he lost his leg in the war. Damn cripple, that's what he is. I should throw him out on his ear, let him beg on the streets, or move into a VA hospital. . . . But there's a knot inside of me, in the pit of my ulcerated stomach, something that forces me to keep him at home, feed him, carry him to bed, shave him, clean him. That old bastard is the reason I've never married, too. Who could live with that lunatic, besides me? . . . Another drink, Speedo, make it straight Daniel's this time. . . . What a damned useless life. Someone should invent another way out besides suicide, but the Pope . . ."

(Pitts)

". . . the mess they made. Ruined the felt on my billiard table with stains, and if it's one thing J. B. Pitts don't like, it's brown stains on that smooth green table. My caroms haven't been the same since. But if I've said it once I've said it twice, you can't teach an old dog new tricks. After all, when you gotta go, you gotta go. . . . Say, Barcheap, plug the frickin' hole, and if the phone's for me, tell 'em MR. Pitts cannot be disturbed.

(Malone)

". . . would probably declare that a sin, too. Useless, this life of mine. Maybe the old fart will die soon."

At that, Malone stopped talking and began to drink

seriously, glass after glass of Jack Daniel's best. I knew the routine well enough; it was repeated every afternoon for my benefit. He would drink in silence, ignoring J. B. Pitts and his carpetbag of worn-out phrases, until he passed out, facedown on the bar. This always presented me with a bartender's dilemma, as it is illegal in California to have a customer facedown on the bar.

And while Malone grew more and more melancholy, Pitts kept right on talking about Bozo and Lady, then about the price of coffee, then lamenting the fact that you can't get good help these days, which was another subtle request for a refill. "You call that a drink? Hell, that wouldn't satisfy a hummingbird in the Sahara Desert. I demand to see the manager. You can't underpour J. B. Pitts and get away free as a lark. I bring more business into this place than the freeway. . . ." On and on, laughing at his own jokes, replying to his own questions, lining up lemon twists for the inevitable moment when he would challenge my estimate of what he owed.

"And don't forget the receipt, Barcheap. J. B. Pitts never took a handout in his life. . . ." On and on.

A busboy came into the bar from the adjoining kitchen and whispered a few words in Pitts' ear, returning to the kitchen a few dollars richer. Pitts looked up at me, winked as he drank, and murmured another favorite: "A nod is as good as a wink to a blind bartender!"

Every day, Jésus, the busboy, risked his job for those dollars by hiding bucketsful of ribs in the locker room until that certain moment when he would sneak them into the trunk of J. B. Pitts' blood-red Cadillac, for the St. Bernards back home. He was eventually fired for this illicit practice, and subsequently hired by J.B., but that is another story.

"Yessir, a nod is as good as a wink. What the boss don't
know can't hurt him, eh, Barcheap? And that boy, Heysoos,
knows not to bite the hand that feeds his eleven kids. . . . Say,
Barcheap, are you ever going to do something about this hole
in my glass?"

I gave J.B. another Ballantine and water, refilled
Murphy's glass with Jack Daniel, and wondered to myself
when the liquor would have its well-known side effect. Taking
his cue from my thoughts, or so it seemed, J.B. excused himself to the john with his bathroom exit line that we all knew
so well.

"Got to go to the Summer Room," he invited.

"Summer Room?" I responded perfunctorily, awaiting
his ritual reply as I made a fresh pot of coffee.

"Yessir, Summer for Boys and Summer for Girls!"
laughing his way through the swinging doors, not forgetting
to put a napkin over his drink to tell the world that J. B. Pitts
would be back.

During Pitts' absence, Malone looked at me with his
basset-hound eyes and mumbled something like "Nothing to
be done. . . ." Then he passed out, forehead slamming down
onto the bar with a painfully noticeable thud. Murphy
Malone had done it again. I sighed, thinking about his
manner of getting drunk. He was one of those rare customers
who remained completely sober until he fell unconscious.
Years of bourbon had destroyed his liver, prematurely
grayed his hair, and wrinkled the forehead that now lay flat
on the bar, but in all those years Murphy Malone's speech
had never slurred, he had never staggered in the semi-
balanced manner that drunks in the movies are known for, or
killed himself on the highway. One night I counted forty-
seven manhattans, consumed in groups of five at a time, but

even then he was sober until the lights went out. His last line that night was "She sells sea shells by the seashore," without a mistake. I sighed again and poured him a cup of coffee.

When Pitts had relieved himself (or grown too lonely in the john while trying) he returned to the bar and ordered a round for the house, a dubious gesture since he was the only one drinking. He had forgotten for the moment his napkin-covered glass of receipts. That was J. B. Pitts' manner of getting drunk: talking louder and forgetting. The more Ballantine he consumed, the more he forgot, often leaving his wallet, derby, and cane at the bar to be retrieved by his faithful wife later in the evening.

His exits, when finally they came, were always colorful in comparison to the weak-kneed disappearing act of his silent partner in the green tuxedo. After demanding a kiss from the cocktail waitress, to whom he always referred as Marilyn Monroe, he would nudge the unconscious Malone next to him, saying, "Better dead than Red, eh, Maloney, you old Irish poop?" Finally, after lining his lemon twists domino-fashion across the bar, he would announce his coming intention to depart with another of his barroom clichés.

"Front and center, Barcreep. Fix me a roadrunner!"

"What's a roadrunner?" I ask, after pretending to look up the recipe in *Old Mr. Boston's Bartending Manual.*

He would glance around the cocktail lounge, check that he had everyone's attention, then bellow, "Why you stupid egghead, that's one for the road!" Then he would laugh and laugh.

"Don't you try and give me a fox, now. No sir, Barcreep, you can keep the fox. Just give me the roadrunner without the fox and I'll be on my way home to the love of my life."

I always wondered whether J.B. was speaking of his

wife or of the St. Bernards when he repeated the affectionate phrase. After all, he didn't have pictures of his wife in his wallet, only photos of Bozo and Lady.

Four or five roadrunners later, minus a random derby and cane, J. B. Pitts would find some reason to withhold my tip as he staggered out of the bar, saying, "Just check the lemon if you don't believe me. Yep, if only them lemons could talk ..."

Once in the parking lot, after fumbling all-thumbs with his keys, he would drive his blood-red Cadillac full of stolen barbecued ribs to Bozo and Lady. Eventually the taxi would come for Murphy Malone, and while Marilyn Monroe would start lighting the candles and Jésus refilled the ice bin, I would start cutting lemon twists for the evening shift.

OUTCAST STATE
by Thomas Cody

The blurred faces were jumping around like Chinese lanterns. The words forming the question came from the first row, but he couldn't immediately tell who spoke them.

"I asked about 'I all alone beweep my outcast state,' Mr. Joiner," the voice repeated.

He steadied his gaze, searching out the faces in the first row, and coming to rest on Susan. He should have known. Eager, unflinching Susan, forever probing beneath the surface of the written word.

He took a deep breath and ran his tongue over the roof of his parched mouth to free it from dryness.

"When Shakespeare says, 'I all alone beweep my outcast state,' Susan"—he hesitated while he tried to think out the words he wanted—"he is talking about those who are shunned by society, those who in popular terminology are called the losers. We all know them—the drifters, the debtors, the lonely, the drunkards, the . . ." he tried to recall the word but it was too late.

Did it really make any difference? he wondered. Surely they all knew by now. The trembling hands, halting speech, the bloodshot eyes and flushed look—they had seen the signs often enough.

He continued: ". . . men who are alone, shut off from the rest of society for one reason or another, with no one to pity them, and so they must pity themselves."

The longed-for ringing of the bell sent the blurred faces shuffling out of the room, and as they left he whispered to himself a thankful, "Good-bye shadowy faces and good-bye Mr. Shakespeare, at least until Monday morning."

The first two drinks went down with difficulty, but after that a velvety smoothness took over, and for the first time that day he started to feel alive.

It was half past four, and she would soon arrive. He pictured her movements from the time she had finished her tour of duty at four o'clock. By five minutes after four she had been in the bar around the corner from the police station, having her first whiskey. If it had been a quiet day, she had water with her whiskey; if things had gone wrong, beer had been the chaser.

Halfway through the drink she had started to relax, exchanging small talk with the bartender while having a second drink. Then she had gotten on the bus outside the bar for the ten-block ride, getting off two blocks from the bar he was in.

Arriving, she ordered a beer with her whiskey, and he knew she was in a bad mood. As she emptied the glass, the lines around her mouth and under her eyes deepened, the alcohol-dried skin sagged, and he could see her lower lip tremble on the glass.

Had he ever really loved her? he asked himself. He thought back to the time they had started going together, back seven years. They had been introduced at an American Legion dance, and they had hit it off right away. Certainly there had been a strong mutual attraction, both enjoying the same things—dancing, the theater, reading, and lively conversation over drinks.

Their mutual likes had carried them through the year and a half until they married. During that time they had planned everything so confidently, certain that nothing could mar their plans. After two years of marriage they would have enough money saved to buy a small house. Then there would be the children—at least three, they both agreed. He was going to study for the assistant principal's examination; it was a difficult test, but with her and the children to work for he knew he could pass it.

Yes, it had all seemed so simple, what could possibly go wrong? But many things did go wrong.

After the first hectic weeks of marriage, when their lives settled into a routine of quiet boredom, they realized they had made a mistake. The blame wasn't his or hers. They both understood that; and with the silent forebearance with which most people accept their blunders, they attempted to make their marriage manageable.

They tried to bring some order into their lives, but her job as a policewoman made it difficult because she was required to work different shifts. Sometimes she finished work at four in the afternoon; other times she finished at midnight or at eight in the morning.

For days on end they saw each other only briefly, until

they became like strangers who shared nothing but the same apartment. Their sexual relations became less and less frequent, until now their only indulgence took place when both were in such a drunken stupor that they were hardly aware of their awkward fumblings.

Since they found each other bearable only when they were drinking, alcohol assumed an all-important place in their lives. The pleasures they had found in the theater and dancing gave way to the comfort they found in drink.

His preparation for the assistant principal's examination stopped. All study and reading became irksome drudgery, and for the first time in his ten years of teaching he began to dread facing his classes. He did less and less actual teaching and resorted to busywork, having his students read chapters from their textbooks and answer the questions at the end of each chapter.

Two years after their marriage, she had become pregnant and along with her pregnancy came a renewal of hope for them. By tacit, mutual consent they cut down sharply on their drinking; they started saving money for the house that now came back into their plans, and he returned to studying for the assistant principal's examination.

One night while on duty at the station house she had to subdue a drug-addicted prostitute. She had been knocked down and kicked, and the miscarriage that resulted shattered their brief period of hopefulness.

Drink became more important than ever, and each seemed determined to outdrink the other. Their savings were soon dissipated, and they went into debt to satisfy their craving for alcohol.

A year after her miscarriage he had a heart attack. While he was in the hospital, the doctor told him that he had high blood pressure and that he would have to give up drinking. The realization of his mortality shocked him, and he decided to follow the doctor's advice. When he came out of the hospital he assumed the role of guardian to her, meeting her after her tour of duty and sitting long hours in bars, sipping ginger ale while she drank her whiskeys.

She would say nothing to him until she had finished four or five drinks; then she would tell him about her tour of duty, about the pickpockets, exhibitionists, prostitutes, and drug addicts with whom she had come in contact. Finally the accumulation of the day's and night's drinking freed her from all inhibitions, and she would turn on him, calling him all the vile names that were common to her job and taunting him to take a real drink.

He felt himself in the role of a minor martyr, and the role soon began to appeal to him. He felt that all her abuse was his penance. He wasn't certain what he had done to require penance, but he had a vague, uneasy feeling that somehow he was guilty for the failure of their marriage.

For three months he had played his sweet-suffering role; then one night she became particularly brutal in her vituperation, and she threw a drink in his face, telling him it was the only way he would ever again take a real drink.

As he wiped his face with his handkerchief, he tasted the sharp bite of the alcohol. It had been an extremely difficult day at school, and his nerves were beginning to wear thin. He told the bartender to bring him a double whiskey.

Sitting next to her now, he could tell she was relaxed. She turned to him, smiling, and he could hear the barely audible sigh that meant the day's tensions had been temporarily defeated. From his change on the bar she took two quarters and went to the jukebox. He knew just which numbers she was about to play and he could already hear her first words when she sat down again: "Let's liven up this joint a bit; it's like a morgue in here." He emptied his glass and nodded to the bartender for a refill.

It was going to be a long Monday. Beads of perspiration were seeping through his clothes and dripping from his forehead onto the page in front of him. Not daring to talk much, he had told the class that he had to get some important information ready for the office and he had written an assignment on the board. Now he was pretending to copy items from a month-old dental inspection sheet, but on the paper he had scrawled the words, *"whiskey, soothing whiskey, warming whiskey, welcome whiskey."*

From the right side of the room came a suppressed giggle, and he was certain that he heard the word "drunk." He didn't dare look up, trying instead to concentrate on the scrawled words on the dental sheet, but they had turned into indecipherable objects. They reminded him of a Miró painting. The thought amused him, and he broke into a laugh.

He looked more intently at the scrawls, and now he saw that they actually were parts of a Miró painting. Fascinated, he watched as the small, wobbly word objects curved from one side of the paper to the other, forming weird geometric patterns.

As he continued watching, the slimy, crawling word-insects started moving to the top of the sheet. When they reached the top they didn't stop, as they were supposed to, but kept crawling. Now they were on his hands and starting up his arms.

He tried to brush them off, but it was no use; they kept

wriggling up and up, and now they passed from his arms to his body. Frantically he tried to brush them back onto the sheet, but they slipped through his flesh as if there were no material substance to his body.

They kept coming, more and more of them, in a never-ending swarm, and he jumped up from his chair, crashing it to the floor.

Shouting at the top of his voice, he begged the slimy insects to let him alone, to return to the dental sheet and be words again. But he knew they wouldn't stop, that it was no use shouting.

He ran to the blackboard, throwing himself against it for protection. His nails screeched across the slate, and rivulets of tears streamed crookedly down the board.

The hand on his shoulder seemed to offer further protection, and he turned from the board. Mr. Hanson, the principal, had an understanding expression on his usually stern face, and even though the words he spoke had no meaning, the tone was soothing.

As Mr. Hanson led him from the room, the young faces peering at him were curious but not unkind. What could he say to them? He tried to recall some familiar lines that might somehow sum it all up, but he could think of nothing. He smiled at them, hoping they really did understand.

A NEW LIFE
by Patricia Sieck

Hank Spiller waited for the elevator that would take him to his parking level. A crowd was waiting with him. They milled in front of the closed door eyeing the red number above the door—the elevator had stopped at the third floor for several seconds.

An overweight, pants-suited woman pushed the button that summoned the lift. She was the fourth person to have done so. We're all tired, Hank thought, I'm not the only one who's had a long day. Others in the crowd looked at their wrists and shook their watches to be sure they hadn't stopped.

Hank considered the advertisements that lined the walls, vying for people's attention. There was a picture of a family in front of a white cottage set in a very green yard. The family was smiling its security to the restless group. The parents stood protectively behind the children, holding their small shoulders lightly. He glanced away as the elevator dropped to their floor and he entered.

A New Life

He'd been late this morning; his car was on the fifth floor in one of the last spaces left at ten-thirty A.M. As he fitted the key in the door he could see his reflection in the car window. He needed to lose weight; there was a crease where his chin line had been once, and below that a new soft chin. He opened the door and sucked in his pauneh. He was a stocky man in his middle forties and the paunch was partially concealed by the neat gray suit he was wearing. He threw his briefcase in the back seat and settled behind the wheel. The feeling of being a settled businessman pleased him; no one had noticed his late arrival this morning; the new job was going well.

He had skipped lunch. With no drinks and no lunch he would soon lose weight. He hadn't accepted offers to stop for a drink before going home, and he enjoyed the idea of sitting in the apartment after dinner playing with the kids for a while, reading and talking, and then going to bed early. He would tell Clare that things were going to be different, and the thought of it was good.

Perhaps the little house in the advertisement would be worth thinking about—should be more room for the children to grow in, and he could garden the way his father had. Starting over again would be easier in a new place; he could make Clare realize that the past was all over and she would stop bringing it up for every little thing.

He backed the car out and started down the ramp, his mind still on the new life that he and Clare would lead. He'd soon be making good money, and he'd turn it all over to her to handle. They'd save a little and maybe take a trip in the summer; Clare had wanted to see Yosemite ever since they'd come West.

He drove west along California Street with his window down and his elbow resting on the frame. What he wanted was something to drink. A glass of water would be fine, a soft drink even better. He decided to stop at a party store and buy a case of low-calorie pop. His eye caught a bright neon liquor store sign, and he found a parking place half a block away. As he walked down the street, Hank almost collided with a thin man coming toward him. Both Hank and the tall, thin man stepped to one side and then the other, each gesturing and smiling that the other should have the right of way. Finally the tall man stopped looking at Hank's feet, and a surprised smile of recognition crossed his face.

"Hank, you old son of a gun!" He stopped his dancing and held out his hand. "I'll be damned. It's been five years—that night at the Jade Club when Clare got so mad—" He stopped and made a slightly embarrassed wave with his hand, and then recovered his composure. "Jim said he saw you recently. I was going to look you up before I left town again."

"Good to see you, Bill." Hank stepped out of the way of a woman trying to pass them. "We're blocking traffic. How about a drink? Little tavern right down the way."

The night was damp with a sharp wind sweeping the streets. They walked past the liquor store and around the corner, where a tube of neon outlined a cocktail glass. Hank pushed Bill ahead of them as they entered.

The bartender wiped the counter off and stood expectantly. "I'll have a beer," Hank said. He turned to Bill and offered an explanation. "I'm on the wagon these days. Been overdoin' it—don't feel as good as I could." Bill was understanding and did not argue. He merely ordered a bourbon and water for himself.

They sat drinking slowly and talking of the life they had known—the small-town high school they had attended, the fraternity at college, the years they had both been salesmen for the same firm. They would sit watching their glasses for a moment, and then one of them would laugh and look up.

"Remember the night we got Ronnie what's-his-name drunk? He'd never had a drink before, and you cried in your beer the rest of the night because you said he had to write a paper for you the next day!"

"Sure, I wasn't going to get kicked out of school for a joke." Hank laughed. "Huh, Mother was sure proud of those papers—told people what a great student I was. Clare found out about it after we were married and claimed it was a dirty trick to cheat my own mother." He chuckled and turned his glass around. "She never did understand how to handle Mother. I always did what would make her happy." They both shook their heads and drained their glasses.

Hank looked around for the bartender and then seemed to remember something. "Hey, why don't you come up to the apartment and see Clare and the boys? You haven't got anything important. We'll buy some shrimp and fry 'em. ..." Hank paid for their drinks, and they walked out into the night.

They bought beer and a bottle of bourbon. Hank thought of buying soda pop but decided they had enough to carry as it was. He would do that tomorrow. It had begun to rain in soft, misty drops, and the streetlights were haloed and dimmed. They hurried across the street to a fish market that was closing for the night. Back in the car, they talked and laughed a little less.

The apartment building was of dirty red brick and an electric light shaped like a lantern hung over the door. They pushed into the foyer, and Hank leaned against a buzzer.

"This isn't a bad building—Clare says she lived in one

just like it when she was little. I was thinking tonight, though, that we ought to get a larger place, something in the suburbs maybe— Here, hold this bag a minute. . . . Something seems to be wrong with the buzzer. Think I've got a key."

Hank felt in his pocket and pulled out a key chain with several keys on it. He opened the door to the stairwell and held it open for Bill. The elevator door stuck, and when it finally closed after them Hank just missed catching his fingers in it. Hank pushed a button and they rose noisily to the third floor. Then they walked down a long hall to the door marked 313. The carpet in the hall was dark and had a musty smell during the rainy winter months. In spots it had worn through to the wood. He turned the door handle, but the lock clicked in place as he pulled on it.

"Don't know how you're supposed to get in around here. All the doors locked. . . . Clare must have heard another prowler story or something." He pushed against the door and then rapped and called, "Hey, Clare." The door remained closed.

"Here we go again," he said, as he handed Bill his package and brought out the keys once more.

The door opened easily, and they entered a dark hall much like the one they had just left. The only light in the apartment was reflected from the street below. Hank flicked a switch. A light in the middle of the ceiling illuminated the living room starkly. A glass half full of water stood near a small ivy plant, and a newspaper, opened to the funny papers, lay on the floor. Hank opened a swinging door, which exposed a small kitchenette; they put their bags on the counter and Bill looked at Hank expectantly.

"Guess they've gone out. . . . Must be a note around here

somewhere." He nodded toward the icebox. "There's ice in there—set yourself up. I guess I'll just stick to beer." He opened a can and put the rest of the beer in the refrigerator. It was lucky he had thought to buy shrimp; the shelves were nearly bare.

He wandered around the empty living room carefully, looking behind the table in case the note had slipped off. Bill came in with a tumbler of bourbon. "Here's to you," he said, lifting the glass in salute.

"Must've gone to a late movie and haven't realized what time it is." Hank sat down on one of the cheaply slipcovered chairs and drank deeply.

Bill lit a cigarette and said, "Must've."

The conversation did not pick up, and they sat in silence. Finally, Hank suggested that they make their own meal.

Before they started frying the shrimp, they each got a new drink. Hank laughed more than was his custom after only three beers, but his eyes had a listening look. Every once in a while he would touch Bill's arm and they would both listen to steps in the hall, but the steps either stopped short or went on past the door. They bumped into each other often in the small kitchen, and the fat for the shrimp almost burned. The kitchen was cluttered with dishes, and when they had put the meal together,they went to the dining table in the living room.

Hank set his plate on the table and turned toward the bedroom door. "I'll just take a look at what clothes Clare wore—maybe she's downtown." He opened the door and turned the dressing table light on.

The table stood empty under the light. Dust and powder covered the top in a thin layer, and two bobby pins lay on it.

Hank stood with his hand on the switch; he noticed that it was trembling. Without looking in the closet, he flipped the switch off.

"Pretty good meal, huh?" Hank said, pushing the shrimp around his plate. "We haven't lost the old touch." His voice tried to assume its old spirit. Bill looked at him questioningly. "I guess they're at her sister's."

"Uh." Bill picked up a shrimp in his fingers and ate it, tail and all.

Hank's eyes were watering, and he bit the shrimp meat off and put the tails back on his plate. The conversation was stiff again as they ate and had another round of drinks. Even Bill had begun to start at noises in the hall, but he didn't say anything more.

The telephone rang and they both jumped at the noise. Hank set down his beer can and jovially called, "Just a second" to the ringing phone. "They've kept us waiting long enough, huh?"

He winked at Bill. The hallway was dark, and he brushed against the phone table. He sat down on the bench and picked up the receiver.

"Yeah?" he questioned, waiting for Clare's explanation.

"Is Tony there?"

Hank picked up a pencil on the phone table and made little circles on the dark finish. "You must have the wrong number. This is 866-3260."

Hank hung up.

"Wrong number," he said as he picked up the empty beer can and tried to get a swallow from it.

"Yeah, I heard." Bill looked at the drink in his hand and

finished it in a couple of gulps. "I got to be going. Big deal tomorrow. Got to get an early start."

"I'll drive you to your car."

"No, no." Bill looked out the window, draining the last drops from his glass. "It's not raining. Walk will do me good."

Hank let it go at that. He was anxious to be alone.

Bill picked the last shrimp off his plate and chewed it carefully. The tail crunched loudly in the silence. "Sorry I couldn't see Clare again. Be sure to tell her hello for me."

"Sure. Well, they'll probably be home pretty soon. I'll call her sister and see if she's over there." Hank stood up and punched Bill lightly on the arm. "You give us a call next time you're in town. You've got to see those boys of mine; they'll be bigger than I am pretty soon. Here, I'll give you our number."

"That's okay. You're in the phone book, aren't you?"

They walked to the door, both reaching for the handle at the same time. Hank won, and he ushered his guest out.

"I'll be seeing you around for sure," Bill said. He touched his friend briefly on the arm and moved quickly down the hall.

Hank closed the door and walked to the telephone table. He picked up the receiver and then set it back on the cradle. His hands were shaking again. He could hear a telephone ringing in an apartment down the hall.

Dirty plates and empty beer cans cluttered the table. He carried them into the kitchen. A fork tipped on the edge of a plate, but he managed to carry it as far as the sink before it slid off with a clatter. The kitchen still smelled of grease; the lard they had fried the shrimp in was hardening. Little pieces of batter floated in the center, where it was still liquid.

He glanced at the spot on the shelf where the clock stood;

it had belonged to Clare's grandmother. Now there was a dark mark on the shelf where it had been. The faucet was dripping and he turned the handle tighter. The drip diminished, but it was still there. He turned the faucet on full pressure; the water splashed in the sink and splattered on his suit. He turned it down and filled the glass Bill had used. The water was cold and tasted of chlorine. He poured half of it out and filled the glass to the rim with bourbon.

As he sipped the drink, he picked up the salt and pepper shakers and placed them over the spot where the clock had been. He poured the grease into a can and put the can into the garbage. He made a start on stacking and rinsing, but gave up. The drink was warm, but Bill had used all the ice. He pushed the swinging kitchenette door off the doorstop and shut the messy kitchen from sight.

The paper was still on the floor. He sat down and read an article on unusual storms in the Midwest. The light wasn't good; he needed bright light to read these days. He folded the paper, carefully matching the edges, and put it in the magazine holder.

The hall had grown still. He held a mouthful of bourbon and then swallowed it. It burned in his stomach, but that didn't stop him from finishing the drink and making himself a new one. Sitting, listening. "Should be home soon," he said to no one. The voice was strange in the quiet room and Hank switched on the TV set.

"This is your eleven o'clock news," a swinging voice announced. Hank was surprised. "Late," he said, again aloud. He thought of watering the ivy plant since there was a glass of water next to it, but decided Clare had probably watered it just before leaving.

He picked up the bourbon bottle and carried it into the

bedroom. The room smelled of Clare's perfume, and the long light from the living room touched the empty dressing table.

Hank put the bottle and glass on the night table. He took off his jacket and laid it on the bed and pulled his necktie off. He sat on the edge of the bed, staring at the floor, willing himself to look in the closet. There was no need to turn on the light; his eyes had adjusted to the dark. He saw the closet door with the shoe bag on it. There was only his old pair of tennis shoes and his other brown oxfords. The bag tilted at an angle with the unbalanced weight.

He walked over to the dressing table and blew on the forgotten powder and unlatched the window and opened it wide. The damp mist sucked the sweet odor from the room.

Hank Spiller took off his shoes and lay down on the bed. He lit a cigarette and picked up his drink from the table. He was dreaming about what might have been; he was no longer listening for footsteps.

THE
STUTTERING
HAND

by Kevin O'Cahan

Sergeant Joseph Murphy was drunk. Come to think of it, that wasn't at all unusual since Sergeant Murphy was nearly always drunk. He would refer to it as his occupational hazard. "Drinking is me occupation, and being drunk is the hazard," he would say as he sat in his favorite corner of the bar, puffing forlornly on his pipe. Occasionally he would have to interrupt his occupation to attend to a fit of coughing and wheezing, while silent eyes of other drinkers exchanged messages of sympathy. "Poor Sergeant, that cough is going to kill him someday if the booze doesn't get him first." Then with one grating finale, he'd reach for his glass, muttering, "Must have a wee drop for my sore throat, 'twill ease the cough."

Murphy was not really a sergeant. He had been one a long time ago in the Marines, and it was his lengthy reminiscences about his service that had earned him the rank in later years. In truth, Murphy was a nothing, a bum, a rummy, and all kinds of other euphemisms for what he really was—an alcoholic. True to form, he hadn't held a job for ten years and he eked out an existence of sorts by bumming from his friends, panhandling, and occasional shoplifting. . . .

What *is* this, trusty typewriter? What are we building up to? This story is beginning to sound like some kind of Victorian temperance sermon. Away with demon rum, my friends. Look at poor Sergeant Murphy, once a man, now a vegetable. This is the fate of those who drink. Throw out the bottle before it's too late.

Well, it looks like another futile day. Up early this morning, a trifle hung-over admittedly, but nonetheless full of ambition to write the best short story ever to come out of San Antonio. Shaving with my sleek Trac II, I try to imagine those tiny tough hairs on my chin receding after the first slice only to be caught short and cut shorter by the inevitable second blade. Weighty stuff. Then it comes to me, out of the fog of my sore brain—"Sergeant Murphy was drunk. Come to think of it, that wasn't at all unusual since Sergeant Murphy was nearly always drunk."

Eureka! A magnificent opening line for a great story on the perils of alcoholism. Explore the sad, futile world of the bum. Morning meditations by the sink can yield great things.

So I whip through an inadequate breakfast of cold enchiladas and slightly turned milk, which has the effect of making my hangover a little larger. But the work must be done. Catch the inspiration before it expires.

The clean white page is rolled in and ready to go. "Hello," it says, "got any good words for me today?" Do I ever!

Funny, when it's typed, that opening sentence looks a little bland and definitely overused. But I press on and set the scene for my unfortunate character. Two hundred words later, it's all over. Washed out. A dissipated plot.

Somewhere in the corner of my room there's a bushel of dissipated plots. Every one of them has failed for the same reason—unfamiliarity with the character or the scene. They teach this at writing schools all over the world: "Write from experience." Will I ever learn?

Let's face it, I'm not a rummy. I don't even know any members of this special social class. Sure, I've seen them downtown, I've even been approached for "coffee" money. But I can't write about the feelings, emotions, and environment of skid row. I'm not an alcoholic.

So, Sergeant, it looks as if the chronicle of your sad life will have to remain untold. There's no O. Henry Award in this one. Anyway, this hangover's getting worse. I think it's time for a hair of the dog. I realize it's a little early in the morning for a snort of scotch, but it certainly seems to stabilize the corpus fragilis.

Big Mr. Finnegan of the stuttering hand. It's germane even if my name is Mike not Tim, Lannigan not Finnegan. The stuttering hand, however, is a characteristic of many Irishmen. My country, God save us, has the dubious distinction of having more teetotalers per capita and more alcoholics per capita than any other nation that cares to keep such records. The horrifying conclusion, of course, is that those who drink certainly make up for those who don't.

As a boy in Dublin, I was coerced, like many others, into membership in the Pioneers. This is not some Outward Bound group. No, sir, it's the Pioneer Total Abstinence Association. It does not mean abstinence from everything, but total abstinence from alcohol. "Total" seems irrelevant—after all, abstinence is abstinence.

The Stuttering Hand

We gathered for confirmation in the Pro-Cathedral. In a typical Irish paradox, Dublin, a bastion of devout Catholicism, lacks a Roman Catholic cathedral. It does, however, have two Protestant cathedrals, legacies of centuries of English rule. As part of the confirmation ceremony, the local archbishop had us recite "the pledge," a solemn promise to abstain forever. Shortly afterward, he probably retired to the nun's convent down the street for a glass or two of sherry.

The more cosmopolitan of us, and I was certainly one of those, mouthed the pledge in case anyone was watching our lips, but said not a word. Afterward, we congratulated one another on our minor rebellion. We didn't know what we were rebelling against, but all the signs said that when grown-ups drank they had a jolly time, and we didn't want to miss out on that. For our pledge we received a pin of the Sacred Heart of Jesus enameled on finest Cork foundry brass. This we should wear proudly on our lapel to show the strength of our belief. What the heart of Jesus had to do with it I'm not sure, but those of us in the rebellion mysteriously lost our pins shortly thereafter.

My parents drank, my God how they drank. But in a genteel manner—not in public bars but in the quiet of our home and often in the privacy of their bedroom, where other strange things were rumored to take place. My first drink was on my eighth birthday, when, after too much partying (of the childlike kind), I became sick. My father prescribed "Paddy's Panacea," the Irishman's cure for all ills—neat Irish whiskey. I promptly returned it in projectile fashion over his shirt front. He was horrified at the waste of such liquid gold.

I hear footsteps outside. Someone is climbing the last step to my garret. A visitor, ye gods, and me with dirty dishes in the sink and the bed unmade. Perhaps a comely woman seeking my body. Perhaps a collection agency. Perhaps . . .

The sergeant's problem had started about fifteen years ago when he got himself involved (as the saying goes) with a tempestuous bitch of a red-haired woman. A weak man, insecure, and badly in need of love and affection, Joe Murphy could not resist the enticements of a woman who really seemed to care about him. What she was looking for, of course, was shelter and money to support her drinking habit. Joe's friends tried to warn him off, but have you ever tried to cool a person in love? All he could see was the warmth of her smile and the tenderness of her touch. She was no beauty, God knows, but to Joe she was Venus reborn. The affair was short and vicious and left a shattered man in its wake. A man who turned back to the very weakness of his temporary lover. Booze became his consolation.

In time he forgot her, but he had a new and more poisonous attachment that began to dominate his life. As penance for an unhappy few months of passion, he had been sucked into the cesspool of life because of his inability to cope with the loss of a woman he thought he loved. . . .

Now I ask you, isn't that a bit much? "Cesspool of life"—really! What kind of moralistic crap is this, anyway? It's bad enough that I don't have the experience, without coming on like a Pharisee from North Carolina.

It's been three days since I last attempted the saga of Joe Murphy, at least that's what the calendar says. But I seem to be unable to recall at least one of them. I have certainly come closer to the Joe Murphys of this world, but it doesn't seem to have helped any. Mind you, the aftereffects of the last few days are also taking their toll.

Remember the footsteps? That moment of suspense as someone approached my door? Well, it was Virginia. Lovely, lusty Virginia Sherry, one of my closest friends, an occasional lover and boozing companion.

"Hello, Mike sweetie. What's new? Getting much?"

"I'm not getting much work done, but I'm sure that's not what you mean. Glad you staggered along, though. We need some bloody sanity around here. Want a drink?"

"Jeez, Mike, it's only ten o'clock. This is no time for drinking. It's time for . . ."

"Yes, I know, Virginia. Is that why you came?"

"Perhaps," she said coyly, moving around on her tour of inspection as familiar girlfriends (or nosy ones) usually do. I viewed her appreciatively. Pert, slim, with short raven hair, she exuded a primal sexuality in every vague movement. Her tiny breasts—no *Playboy* udders here, thank God—pronounced their presence softly behind her thin sweater. Joe Murphy and his fellow bums had made me forget the pleasant kind of bum like that enclosed in Virginia's tight white slacks, which hid not a curve or a ripple. Ah, woman! Thou art sent to torment the righteous writer. As the old-fashioned books used to say (the ones that got past the Irish censors), I felt a stirring in my loins.

"You know, Mike, you drink too much. Did you ever think about that? I drop in on you early in the morning, and there you are with a glass in your hand. Drinking alone, too, not even a social exercise. I worry about you, sweetie. You're going to pickle yourself. You bloody Irish are all the same. Every one of you is a budding Brendan Behan."

"Behan was gay," I retorted angrily. "*That* I'm not. Anyway, what is the *right* time to drink, for Christ's sake? Seems to me you're pretty good at elbow-bending yourself. I suppose you think it's okay if you wait till five o'clock. That's bourgeois, and you know it. And you know, Virginia, I'm drinking this morning for a valid reason"—a brilliant rationalization came to mind—"I'm writing a story about an alcoholic and I'm trying to simulate the experience. So if you don't want to join me, at least lay off the sanctimony."

Virginia's eyes grew cloudy and her chin shimmered slightly as she smiled. Too late, I realized; she had trapped me once more. Raising anger in me was part of her foreplay. It turned her on.

She drew toward me from the west. I did not resist.

Later, a happy couple, we go for lunch. Outdoors by the river, watching the tourists wander along the river walk, now San Antonio's biggest attraction (after the Alamo, that is—always Remember the Alamo). We chatter aimlessly through a couple of frosty martinis, washed down with a liter of tolerable Chablis. It's Virginia's treat, and in the afterglow of the morning's fun, I enjoy. Coffee and cognac is the fitting conclusion.

After, we stroll along the river and wave crazily at the tourists in the puttering water taxis. There's nothing very Irish about San Antonio, but it suits me fine. The weather's good, the company congenial, and it has a beauty unique among American cities.

In the sultry heat of the afternoon, back once more to my overworked bedroom for an active but sweaty siesta. Then it seems natural to go for a few beers, since it's hot and sticky and the thirst is upon us.

Up to this point, it has been a great day. Now, the memory gets cloudy and unpleasant. There is raucousness, shouting, and vulgarity, and scores of ugly, Hogarthesque people wandering in and out of focus. Leering mouths with rotten teeth zooming in on me like spastic camera shots. Halitosis fills the air.

The Stuttering Hand

The tragedy unfolds at the Hacienda Bistro, my local watering hole. We are sitting in a quiet corner with a couple of Lone Stars before us. One thing leads to another and soon we are part of a large group, some friends, mostly strangers. The conversation is probably nonsensical and the singing, I'm sure, is discordant as hell, but it sounds great at the time.

One Mexican couple, whose names I forget, but I'm sure she was Juanita—all sultry Mexican beauties are called Juanita—gets up on the table to dance. In some strange, cultural throwback to Andalusia, they do a passable flamenco, skillfully sidestepping the ashtrays. My strongest recollection of the performance is the view up Juanita's skirt. At least her underwear is clean.

Virginia is enthralled by the performance and wastes no time in expressing her feelings to the male performer. She's like that sometimes. Not exactly a loose woman, but she likes to try something new once in a while. She leaves with him later, no doubt to try her own style of fandango. Juanita seems unconcerned and latches on to some burly fellow who had enjoyed the view of her underpinnings. I try to appear unconcerned, but in truth I'm a little jealous and angry at Virginia for abandoning me with this particular ensemble. But so it goes.

As the night deepens, people come and go. One of those who joins us is an attractive redhead about thirty-five. A little worn around the edges but attractive all the same. In my now highly high state, I realize she is Joe Murphy's lover, the one who had caused him to fall in the gutter (or was it the cesspool) of life when she threw him away. The fact that Murphy is one of my dissipated plots doesn't seem relevant. This woman has ruined my friend and I intend to settle the score.

It must be a ridiculous conversation. Obviously, she doesn't know Murphy, but then she's the kind of woman who can't be absolutely sure. I insult her and abuse her in drunken verbiage as best I can. She throws her drink in my face.

Let's understand one thing. I'm not an arrogant drunk. I'm a happy drinker and I don't get into fights like most of my countrymen. But damn it, I'm annoyed when the beer hits my eyes. I go for her like a wounded lion.

What happened after that is very hazy. I am grabbed, kicked, and pushed and thrown around. I feel pain and pain again. Everything spins around me in wild gyrations as I am evicted. Not violently, mind you, as in "el tipíco" Western movie, but gently propped up against the outside wall with an exhortation to "go home and sleep it off."

Good advice, I think, and in spite of the agony and lack of muscular control, I steer a wavy course homeward. After a few steps my stomach finally rebels at the continued abuse and disgorges its horrible contents on me and the sidewalk. I stagger on and trip on something—maybe my own feet, who knows—and the concrete reaches up to me with alarming speed to switch off my consciousness in one searing blow.

Life returns as I am prodded and slapped on the face. Voices ask questions that I cannot understand. I think I request an early death because that seems to be the uppermost objective. Through the haziness of my eyeballs, there appear to be two policemen above me with disgusted looks on their faces.

' Okay, ya creep. What's yer name?"

"Tim Finnegan, sir, of the stuttering hand," I mumble.

"You'll have stuttering balls if you don't stop being a smart ass. Your name, rummy?"

"Mike Lannigan, sir, pleased to meet you. 'Tis freshly arrived from the Emerald Isle I am."

"Aw, let's not waste time with this one. We'll throw him in the tank. What a bloody mess he is!"

Then I am thrown in the back of a well-named paddy wagon, which bumps its way forever to somewhere.

Yes, I end up in jail in the drunk tank, where they wait for me to sober up. It's a painful period and the agony is still with me. The company is not so hot either—a depressing collection of society's misfits groaning in their own filth as the turmoil of inevitable hangovers tears them apart.

I feel pity and disgust. How could they lead such lives? Then I look at myself sitting there, my clothes covered in cold vomit, suffering the same pains as my cellmates. I am one of them.

Well, Sergeant Murphy, I think I'm ready to tell your story now. Perhaps a new lead would help:

When Sergeant Murphy pried open an eye he smiled a little in spite of his thumping hangover. He was in familiar surroundings, his friendly detox center. . . .

Tomorrow Will (Not) Begin a New Life

WINTER
by Michael B. Brodin, M.D.

One could sense the onset of winter. You exhaled vapors. Today the sky was clear, and the west side of the hospital was yellow bright from the afternoon sun.

The emergency area was to the rear and at this time of the day was in shadow. When John Berman went through the revolving glass doors, the waiting room was only half full. He didn't have to waste time asking directions, he knew exactly where he was going because this was his fourth time. He registered at the desk with the complaint of "abdominal pain and vomiting." That was usually the best way to get the fastest service. He went outside to smoke a cigarette, for he knew that it would be at least two hours before he was seen.

Then he walked to the front of the hospital building, where it was warmer. He could feel the chills and sweats coming on. This time he had timed it just about right, he thought. The anxiety was just starting to make itself felt, the hallucinations just beginning to ease their way into his mind. It seemed to him like rainwater seeping into crevices in the pavement, the way the hallucinations seeped into his brain. And his mental image seemed to be correct, anatomically speaking, for he had once seen a human brain, a real one, shortly after the death of a friend. It was a death for which he felt partly to blame, since he had been driving, blind drunk, while his friend was sleeping next to him. The force of the crash was not itself pronounced, but a sharp piece of metal from the other vehicle had struck the man's skull in such a way as to cleave it in the midline, opening it like a book, exposing the cranial contents. He was surprised at all the foldings and cracks on the surface of the brain, and this image now helped to form his idea of how the "strange" ideas insinuated themselves into his psyche. He scratched an imaginary insect off his nose. Momentarily he thought it was a roach.

He was feeling quite ill. Very weak, very nauseated, very uncomfortable. The fluid had been accumulating in his abdomen, his "beer belly," and it now protruded in a bizarre and hideous fashion. His stools had been black and tarry and foul-smelling. His eyes and skin had been yellow for three or four weeks—he couldn't remember the duration exactly. His memory had long since been bedeviled and confounded. Still, he took his daily fifth. For the past several days, of course, he had taken considerably less and it was this partial withdrawal that was now causing most of the symptoms. But this was the last time. He vowed never again to allow himself to slip.

After his cigarette, he returned to the emergency department. He was too weak to stand outside any longer; he sat and waited his turn. His nausea and anxiety grew stronger. The phantom, fleeting insect hallucinations were becoming more frequent. He thought he saw a spider crawling up his arm, and he brushed it away. He was back to reality for the moment. Two and a half hours passed. He was on the brink of losing control—

"John Berman," someone shouted. It was a nurse standing in a large doorway. He got up and walked toward the entrance to the examining rooms, almost from habit. He remembered well walking through the door and then . . . nothing. Luckily an orderly had been close at hand to break his fall. It was to be expected, actually: a simple "fainting" due to sudden loss of blood pressure from getting up too rapidly. Normally he would have been able to handle it, but since his red blood count was so low he simply did not have enough oxygen to keep his brain functioning.

His first sensation upon awakening was the odor. It had always impressed him the same way before; not the usual antiseptic alcoholic smell one usually associates with hospitals. No, this hospital, especially the ward he was on, was different. The odor was a mixture, an effluvium of sweat, urine, feces, vomit, and blood. And fetor hepaticus, the peculiar mousy smell which characterizes the alcoholic in his cirrhotic stupor. John Berman recognized this odor but could not label it.

"Well, John, back again, eh?"

The voice was familiar. It was the sandy-haired intern who had taken care of him the last time. With blue eyes and tan freckles, Dr. Kelly looked too young to be a physician.

"Hi, Doc, whaddya know?" John wasn't a bad patient, just immature. He listened and understood but couldn't stand pain. He had never known the feeling of accomplishment, of meeting and overcoming pain. He had no tolerance.

"I told you the last time that I thought you'd be back," the doctor said.

"I know, Doc, I know. But this is the last time. I've made up my mind."

"It may be, it just may be. One way or another. We'd better get you worked up now, before we really start having trouble."

John knew that, too. The sooner his physical examination was over, the sooner he would receive the medication that would slow the onset of the delirium. Luckily his history was already part of the hospital records. No need for extensive questioning by the doctor. Neither of them felt up to it, anyway. The routine of the examination was predictable: eyes, ears, nose, mouth, neck, chest–lungs, chest–heart, abdomen, scratching the soles, tapping the knees, little finger in the scrotum, index finger in the rectum. Always the same. Except this time.

"You've really got a lot of fluid in your belly, John. You weigh twenty pounds more than you did three months ago when you were discharged. It's all fluid and it's all in your belly."

John wasn't really concerned. His main worry now was the delusion he had that the doctor was an ape, a grotesque orangutan.

"You've got another problem, too. Your blood count is very low and you've got blood in your stool. It's either an ulcer or varicose veins in the esophagus that are bleeding. We'll have to get some X rays in a few days to see which it is."

"Hey, Doc, I'm thinking. Could you get me a little water?"

"No fluids by mouth, just like the last time. We've got to get you to eliminate the fluid you've got inside you already.

No water. I'll tell the nurses to let you have some ice chips. So long, I'll see you in the morning."

The young doctor turned and walked away briskly. He was beginning to have ambivalent feelings for his alcoholic patients. On the one hand, they were people who had created their own problems, mostly in the face of repeated warnings about the consequences. On the other hand, if you studied them carefully enough, and thought about the problem long enough, you came to the conclusion that they were not in control of themselves.

But what he needed now was sleep. Life and death assumed somewhat less importance. He entered his history and physical findings on John Berman's chart and wrote orders for the nurses to follow. Wearily he went to bed. It was three A.M. and rounds with the chief began at eight.

Sleep overcame both men in time, but to each a very different sort. Whereas Dr. Kelly slid into heavy rest rather quickly, John Berman dozed and waked, fainted and was aroused, heavily sedated, thick-tongued, hallucinating. Bizarre gargoyles, terrible insects, huge and armored, multi-colored, with serrated jaws and dorsal spines, compounded eyes and wings. In and out of the room, crawling on him. Craziness alternating with sanity. Like a switch. On and off; nightmare on, nightmare off. At one point, John felt maggots beneath his eyelids.

It could have been five minutes, five hours, five decades. The sun rose; the doctor was telephoned in order to awaken him, the patient rescued from his terrors by a painful injection of sedative.

John wasn't saved yet. The insanity had not left him. He found himself restrained, shackled to the iron bedposts. He had evidently become violent during the night. He remembered very little. The drugs did nothing but depress the aberrant electrical impulses that flitted like lightning bugs in John's brain. Temporarily, he could expect relief.

Now it was Friday morning, seven fifty-five A.M. Dr. Kelly and Dr. Morris, the other intern on the ward, sat in the conference room with their resident, Dr. Singh. Six medical students stood nearby, younger obviously and less at ease in the hospital. A man entered the room where they had congregated. He was about fifty, distinguished, bespectacled, and well-built.

"Good morning, Dr. Christianson," said Dr. Singh in his British-Indian accent. The interns and medical students stiffened a bit and those who had been sitting stood up in respect for Dr. Christianson, one of the best of the attending internists at the medical school.

And he nodded and smiled to them.

"Nice and brisk this morning. Good walking weather. Is everybody ready?"

In answer they filed out of the room and onto the ward. It was eight A.M.

"How many patients do you have to present today?" Dr. Christianson asked.

"I've got three," Dr. Kelly replied.

"I've got four," said Dr. Morris.

John Berman was the first patient to be presented on rounds that day. He was more or less oblivious to what was going on around him and wasn't fully aware of the presence of the retinue until they had all gathered around his bed. "Mr. John Berman, forty-two-year-old white male, unemployed accountant," Dr. Kelly began.

"Fourth County Hospital admission, chief complaint abdominal pain and vomiting. Present illness—"

"Just a minute," Dr. Christianson interrupted. "I think this would be a good time to exercise the cerebral hemispheres of some of our medical students." He looked at the lone female student. "Miss . . . ?"

"Graeber," she said.

"Miss Graeber, knowing nothing more in the history, tell us all you can about this case by means of inspection and examination."

She smiled at John Berman and immediately grasped his wrist in order to take his pulse.

"The patient looks older than his stated age and is obviously jaundiced."

"How do you know that he isn't yellow from carotinemia, from eating too many carrots?" Dr. Christianson smiled. He was in a good mood.

"Because his eyes—his sclerae, to be precise—are also yellow. This only happens with jaundice."

Dr. Christianson was mildly impressed. "Continue," he said.

"There are numerous spider angiomas of the face and"—she paused to lift up his hospital gown—"of the chest and abdomen as well. There is prominent muscle wasting of the shoulders, arms, and hands. There is palmar erythema and a mild liver flap. The abdomen is protruberant with prominent varicosities. A good example of the caput medusae." She felt the extreme tautness of the yellow abdominal skin. "Probably distended from ascites." She pulled down the sheet that had been covering his groin. "There is a female escutcheon and"—she paused to palpate his testicles—"testicular atrophy as well."

Miss Graeber pulled down the gown and pulled up the sheet in order to cover the patient.

"In summary," the medical student said, "there are all

the classic signs of chronic and excessive alcohol intake, cirrhosis and portal hypertension." She wasn't smug about her knowledge, but approached things in an ordered, logical fashion. The making of an excellent physician.

"Well, Miss Graeber—perhaps I should call you Dr. Graeber—that was a very nice presentation indeed. Let's see if I can embellish slightly on your diagnosis." He had noted the distance in the stare of John, his dreamy look, the alternating anxiety which almost bordered on terror.

"Mr. Berman, please take this string from me." He held his hands as if he were holding a string or cord stretched between them. He moved his hands above Berman's head. Berman looked up, looked and reached for the imaginary string. His hand grasped at the air, but he tried again and again. After the point was aptly demonstrated, the physician withdrew the stimulus.

"Visual hallucinations as a part of the delirium tremens can be accentuated with a little help. Similarly, when things haven't gone too far, it is possible to bring the patient back to reality."

He turned to the patient and addressed him in a commanding tone.

"Mr. Berman," he said. And before continuing, he made sure that the patient had given him what attention it was possible for him to give.

"Mr. Berman, how much alcohol do you consume each day? Whiskey, wine, or beer—things like that?"

John paused, thought.

"Oh, four or five shots a day. Maybe three or four beers. Sometimes less."

"By the way," Dr. Christianson continued, "do you know what day of the week it is?"

John hesitated. "Friday."

"Very good," the attending physician said.

"One more question. How many children do you have?"

"Two. Two girls," John said. There was no hesitation this time.

"Well, Mr. Berman, for their sake, and especially if you want to let them have their father, stop drinking. It's killing you."

The patient said nothing.

As the group walked away, Dr. Christianson turned to Dr. Kelly.

"With that amount of ascites, I'd watch him carefully for esophageal varices. In a day or so I'd get a g.i. man to see him. If he's got significant problems there he could blow out at any time."

Dr. Kelly nodded and made a note on his clipboard.

"Yes, winter will be with us sooner than we think," Dr. Christianson observed.

Afternoons pass slowly in the hospital. The laboratory technicians have finished their rounds and the doctors have finished theirs. John Berman was hallucinating. The effects of the alcohol withdrawal were making themselves obvious. Mostly, the hallucinations were visual and mostly terrible. More than anything in the universe, John Berman wanted to feel the burning pleasure of alcohol upon his parched throat. No matter that the fluid deprivation had left his mouth a desert. It was only alcohol he craved. Or, if not alcohol, just a little water. To all those who passed he cried for water. Some were really there and some were not. He passed the afternoon and evening in a nightmare of twisted and tortured fantasy.

He was restrained again with the heavily padded leather

straps to prevent a serious injury. The violence of the delirium tremens is occasionally severe enough to produce death.

At two A.M. on Saturday, John awoke. He had soaked his gown and sheets with night sweats and urine. He had also defecated. His mental torment had decreased somewhat but had been replaced by a surge of nausea. The stench, he thought, the damned stench. The surge passed. The patient stared out in the semi-darkness, the semi-quiet. He heard sounds of oxygen escaping, of labored breathing, of coughing in the distance. He thought of his wife, divorced now. He couldn't blame her for wanting nothing to do with him. He'd try again, after drying out this time.

He thought of his daughters. They were pretty girls, lucky to take after their mother. He would have to see them as soon as he got out of the hospital.

The nausea struck again, powerful this time, overwhelming, causing the abdominal musculature to contract violently. Projectile bloody vomitus, almost pure blood, some bright red, some like coffee grounds. Another burst, blood projecting onto the bed and onto the floor. The leather restraints prevented him from effectively rolling to one side.

One of the enlarged veins in his esophagus, just above the stomach, had burst. A vessel enlarged to the size of a pencil had ripped open. The blood had filled his stomach and had sickened him, causing the spasms that attempted to expel the noxious conglomerate.

He tried to cry out for help, couldn't. The vomit welled up in his throat. He felt himself choking, as if he couldn't take a breath. He gasped. The matter was sucked into the windpipe, the trachea, and lodged there. Air was unable either to enter or to leave the lungs.

Under these circumstances the loss of consciousness was

rapid. Within thirty seconds the awareness of pain had left. Although the body made some involuntary movements afterward, the brain had become more restful. Complete brain death takes several minutes, but peace is felt long before this.

It was not until a half hour later that the body was discovered. Accidentally. He had died at a time when the nurse was busy elsewhere.

Dr. Kelly was awakened in order to make the formal pronouncement of death. He would also have to inform the family and obtain permission for a postmortem examination. He walked, half asleep, down the stairs and out the door of the house staff residence across the street from the hospital. The wind hit his face and ears. The temperature had gone below freezing for the first time that year. Winter had arrived.

A LONG TIME
UNTIL MORNING

by James Angle

The darkness of the hospital room was almost complete,
except near the windows where a faint glow from a street light
intruded, making a metal bedstead gleam dully. The only
sounds in the ward were the occasional rustle of sheets and
intermittent snores. Charlie Evans lay awake, listening, as he
had for many nights now. The old, familiar tension that
caused him to grit his teeth unconsciously, at a low ebb during
the daytime, still rose from the pit of his stomach during the
nights, keeping him awake.

A harsh, jarring voice from the newcomer's bed suddenly broke the silence, making Charlie start. "Where the hell
am I? What is this place?"

"A hospital, buddy," Charlie said.

"Hospital? What for? I'm not sick."

"Yeah? Looked like something was wrong when they
brought you in this afternoon. You weren't too lively."

"Hell, there's some kind of mistake. I wasn't sick, I was drunk."

"Yeah, I noticed. Don't worry, buddy, you're in the right place."

Charlie heard the rustling of sheets, then a sharp gasp. "What is this? I can't move, I'm tied down!"

"Relax, you're just strapped in bed. They do that when you come in drunk. Just in case you wake up and feel like taking a walk."

"Who are you? What is this place? Damn it, I got to get out of here!"

The sheets rustled again, and Charlie heard the sound of creaking leather. He ground his teeth together; then, realizing what he was doing, forced his jaw muscles to relax. "You might as well stop pulling at those straps. Won't do you any good." Charlie breathed deeply, air hissing through his nostrils. "Think I was a damned nursemaid," he muttered under his breath. Aloud, he said, "If you'll lay quiet for a minute, I'll try to explain."

He lit a cigarette, and the flare of the match briefly illuminated his fleshy face and receding hairline. There were deep vertical frown lines between his eyebrows, and down-turned lines were beginning to form at the corners of his mouth. Although he was only thirty-four, he looked as though he were in his forties. After shaking out the match, he inhaled and continued. "This is an alcoholic ward. You get put in here when your family or whoever's been taking care of you gets sick of picking you up off the streets. Me, I'm voluntary. This is my second time in. Been here five weeks now."

"My God, how do I get out of here?"

Charlie heard a familiar undercurrent of panic in the

voice, but he tried to ignore the sympathy he felt. Forcing a harsh chuckle, he said, "Little thirsty, are you? I know how it is. The first few days are always the toughest." He stopped talking then and lay listening as the newcomer's breathing grew louder. Finally he said, "Ah hell, let's see how you're making out."

As Charlie stood up, he was telling himself, "You'd think I didn't have enough troubles of my own." But still he shuffled barefoot to the newcomer's bed and struck another match, holding it over the bed.

The yellow flame revealed a thin face, beaded with sweat and pale. The young man's mouth was tightly closed, and muscles bulged along his unshaven jaw line as he clenched his teeth. He turned his face to the wall, away from the light, shutting his eyes quickly. "What're you trying to do, blind me?" He kept his face averted for a moment, then slowly turned back to look at Charlie, his eyes squinting. "Hey, you got the run of this place, you can help me. Hell, just a mistake, that's all." He tried to smile, but a twitch in the corner of his mouth marred the effect. As he continued talking, the words came faster and faster. "Just get me loose, and I'll do the rest. That's all, just let me up, and I'll be gone. How about it?"

The match died, and Charlie turned back toward his own bed. His voice was softer than before as he said, "Sorry, buddy, I can't do it. They'd know it was me."

"But Christ, man, I've got to have a drink!"

"Hang on, buddy, you'll make it." Charlie climbed into bed, sighed, and pulled the sheet up to his waist. He lay on his back, his hands clasped behind his head, and tried not to hear the harsh rasp of the young man's heavy breathing, hoping the heavy tranquilizer given the newcomer earlier would take effect again.

Finally the newcomer's breathing slowed and became more regular, and the room was quiet, the quiet punctuated once again by the small sounds made by sleeping patients. Now Charlie listened to see if there would be anything more from the newcomer, hoping he would remain asleep, not wanting to have to listen to any more pleading. "Got enough problems of my own," he muttered as he shifted in bed.

It seemed to Charlie that the dark silence was not broken but only made more intense by soft snores, muted groans, and the creaking of beds. He wondered if anyone else was lying awake in the room, but he thought not; he was the only one, he was alone. Everyone was routinely given sleeping pills, but he had started refusing to take them two weeks before, since they were not strong enough to give him real sleep for more than three or four hours and made him feel groggy the next day.

He turned onto his side and drew his knees up, trying to will himself into the relaxation that would make dozing possible, but his mind kept working. God, love to be out for eight, ten hours. Maybe I ought to go back to the pills. No, no use kidding myself, won't do the trick, booze's the only thing'll do it right. He laughed, but the sound was only a short, soft exhalation. And it'll bitch up a marriage, too, damn it.

His mind turned to the past, and he remembered, or thought he remembered, an idyllic time with his wife, Susan. Had something going there, but booze queered it, he remembered. He thought of an afternoon in his apartment before they were married. Her laughing face had been above him, and the sensation caused by her nipples grazing his bare chest had started a fluttering deep in his stomach. His mouth was dry now with remembered desire. "Christ," he murmured. Then, another time, she lay quietly beside him in the same bed. He remembered her saying calmly, "Charlie, I love you." Memory distorted by wanting assured him that she had meant it, and he thought, God, why'd we have to lose it?

Shifting restlessly in bed, he forced himself to think about the newcomer. Just a kid, really. Can't be more than twenty-five. I was twenty-eight the first time around. Lasted longer than he did.

Charlie started to laugh but stopped suddenly as he thought of the younger man's pale, haggard face. Must have been pretty far gone when they got to him, he guessed. Looked like he'd claw a hole in the wall if he could get loose. Must've been a good long drunk. Yeah, a good, long drunk. Charlie began to sweat. He drew his knees up closer to his body and clenched his fists, muttering, "Jesus Christ, here we go."

A half hour later he rolled over onto his back and straightened his legs. He breathed deeply several times, then threw back the sheet and sat up, swinging his feet to the floor. After wiping his wet forehead with his palm, he lit a cigarette and sat, smoking, wondering how many more cigarettes it would take to bring the morning.

Charlie guessed it was after three o'clock when the newcomer began moaning. First he whimpered, then he started to make a steady humming noise, as if he were forcing the sound through clenched teeth. Charlie knew the sound well, the sound and the kind of dream that went with it. He moved quickly to the young man's bed as the moaning became louder. He rested his hand on the sleeper's shoulder, feeling the muscles twitch and shudder. As he slowly increased the pressure of his hand, he said quietly, "Okay, buddy, okay. It's all right. Come on, wake up now, that's it, buddy, wake up."

The young man stopped moaning, was silent for a moment, then strained against the leather straps that held his arms, trying to move away from Charlie. "Who are you?" he whispered. His breath came quickly and unsteadily.

"Relax, buddy, relax. It's just me, the guy in the ward. You're in the hospital, remember?"

The newcomer sighed shakily, and his breathing began to slow. "Oh, yeah, sure, I remember. Alcoholic ward? What am I doing here?"

Charlie closed his eyes for a moment in the darkness, thinking, Jesus! just like I was. Then he said, "Look, don't try to con me. You know why you're here just as well as I do. Was it a bad one? The dream, I mean."

"Yeah, falling. Didn't think I'd ever stop. My God!" The newcomer's voice had begun to shake again.

Charlie felt a sympathetic tightening within himself. His voice was harsher when he said, "All right, take it easy. There's nothing to get excited about. Just take it easy and ride with it, that's all you can do. And try to keep it down, or we'll have the whole hospital in here."

"Yeah. Yeah, sure."

Realizing that he was holding his arms stiffly at his sides, Charlie forced himself to relax, shrugged, and turned away from the young man. Why me? he thought. Why'd they have to stick him next to me?

As he slipped under the sheet he thought, Yeah, I was a little older than he is. Not much, though. Working at Allen's lot then. He laughed quickly in the darkness as he visualized rows of used cars, new paint jobs and superficial repairs hiding basic flaws. Who'd have thought I'd ever work for that old bastard? Did though, thanks to Susan.

Abruptly, Charlie sat up in bed. "No use, no sense in it,

HAVING BEEN THERE

leave it alone," he muttered. He lit another cigarette and lay back, watching the tiny glow move as his hand trembled.

Unwillingly he remembered that after he had lost his second job in four months, this time for coming to work drunk, Susan had again asked him to go to her father, who had once said that Charlie could always have a job at his Buick dealership. He had refused, almost automatically, and she had said nothing more about it. Then two days later she had come home in mid-afternoon and found Charlie slumped on the living-room couch, a half-empty glass in his hand. She stared at him for a few moments, then sat down in the chair across from him and said, "If you're not too drunk to listen, I have some news."

"Go ahead."

"'I got you a job today. And before you say anything, it's not with Daddy. It's with Bill Allen."

"For Christ's sake, Susan! Allen? That old phony?" Charlie had sat forward quickly, almost spilling his drink.

"Yes, Allen." Her voice was cool, precise. "It's a job, at least, and I had to throw Daddy's name around and let him make passes at me for two hours over lunch before he offered it."

Charlie swallowed hard and pushed himself back against the head of the hospital bed. It would have been so much easier for her just to divorce me, he thought.

He was glad when the sounds of the newcomer struggling against the straps again brought him out of his memories. He had to moisten his lips twice before he could say, "Easy, buddy, easy. You're all right."

The newcomer breathed deeply, then said, "Hey."

"Yeah?"

[152]

"What day is it?"

"Thursday, going on Friday. How long you been drunk?"

"God, I don't know. Four, five days, I guess. I remember things here and there, but most of it's pretty blurred."

The newcomer lapsed into silence, and soon Charlie could tell from the change in his breathing that he was sleeping again. Yeah, he thought, must of been a good one. Sounds like some I've been on. Like the one that landed me here the first time. Must of been a couple of months before I pieced everything together. I knew right away when I sobered up that it had started that night at Allen's house, though. Yeah, I remembered that party, all right. I bitched myself up good that night, that queered everything.

Charlie laughed, a single harsh sound in the dark ward, then said, "I know better than that. It was queered long before that."

He hadn't intended to speak aloud, and the sound of his own voice startled him. He listened, then decided that he hadn't awakened anyone. As his mind returned, unbidden, to a recounting of the earlier time, he unconsciously clenched his fists under the sheet.

They kept asking me if I had a reason, all the doctors and everyone. Hell yes, sure, I had a reason. Those damned people bored me. Hell, they disgusted me. I didn't want to go to the party in the first place, but Susan insisted. We got there late; I wanted to stop for a couple of quick ones on the way, and when we walked in Allen was telling some story. Old Allen, what an ass. He damn near drove me crazy. Always telling some story, and it was always the same one I'd heard the day I started working for him. Same old thing about conning some sucker on a car, unloading a dog. But I didn't listen. I just got myself a drink and started thinking about Susan.

The newcomer started to cough. Charlie could hear, almost feel, the gagging rattle that shook the younger man. Finally the coughing stopped, and as the newcomer gasped for breath, Charlie said, "You okay, buddy? Make it all right?"

"Yeah, yeah, I'm all right. God, I want out of here. Get me out . . . out . . ."

As the voice trailed off, Charlie returned unwillingly to the story that was told and retold in his mind every night.

Yeah, started thinking about Susan. My wife, Susan, sitting right there, eating up every word old Allen said. She figured we'd ought to butter him up that night, like she did when she got me the job. Been on my back for weeks, trying to get me to hit him up for a raise. That's why we were there that night. When she heard he was throwing a party, right away she said, "We're invited, aren't we?"

Told her I guessed we were but I didn't feel much like going. Tried to tell her how much those damned people bored me, but that just set her off. I can still hear her. "Yes, and that's why you don't make any more than you do. We're going to that party, and you're going to get a raise. I'm sick of having to sneak around behind you and ask my folks for things. You ask him tonight, when he's feeling good."

Sitting there at Allen's house, looking at her, I remembered what she'd said. Because it seemed funny, like she was just talking at me, not to me. When I said I didn't know she was getting money from her folks, it was like she didn't hear me. And when I tried to tell her why I didn't want to go, it didn't make any difference to her.

A Long Time Until Morning

Indulging in distorted memories once more, Charlie thought, Used to talk to each other a lot. Like late at night, in bed. We'd talk about plans, and us—and, hell, everything. But that was a long time ago.

He ground his cigarette out in the ashtray, concentrating on killing the last spark. Then he turned his head toward the newcomer's bed, wishing he would wake up again and want to talk—about anything, it didn't matter what. Charlie's hands were shaking more than they had been before, and he clasped them over his stomach to try to stop it.

In the ward's night silence, Charlie's internal narrative continued.

Sitting at that damned party and not listening to the story Allen was telling. Had a good start anyway, from the drink I'd had on the way there, and when I got to looking around, the people all looked funny—all flat-looking, like they were made out of cardboard or something. Old Johnson was there, red hair, fat gut, and all. Bet he's still working for Allen. Johnson, the phony car salesman. Funny, I noticed something about him that night I never paid any attention to before. There were big freckles all over the backs of his hands. Faded, looked almost like the color had started to run on them or something. He was laughing at Allen's story, like he always did, mouth wide open and big stomach shaking. I felt like I could go over and put my fist through that stomach, and he'd keep right on laughing. It scared me, I didn't know what was happening to me.

For a moment Charlie thought he had been speaking out loud, and he wondered if the newcomer was listening to him. Then he shook his head sharply as he remembered that only he could hear this story. The voice inside went on.

Later, I was in the kitchen. Guess it was quite a bit later.

Fixing myself a drink, and the clock on the wall showed midnight. I was trying to figure out what had happened in the last couple of hours, when Allen came in. Right away I thought about Susan, and I knew she'd be hell to live with if I didn't say something to him. Sure didn't feel like it, though. Just the same, I asked him if he didn't think maybe it was time I got a little more money, plus the commissions, since I'd been on the job for six months.

He looked at me awhile, almost like he didn't know me, like he was trying to figure out where I came from. Then he said, "Evans, I've been meaning to talk to you. You know the cars haven't been moving too well lately. I've been thinking it might be a good idea to put someone else out there with you, kind of help put some life in things. Thought I might bring in someone to keep an eye on the whole operation while you and Johnson do a little more selling. That's what you're there for, you know, to unload those heaps."

That really tore it. If it hadn't been for the bourbon, I guess I wouldn't have said anything, but I let him have it. I can still remember the blank expression on his face when I said, "Allen, go screw yourself."

Guess I wanted an honest reaction from him, any reaction, I didn't care what, but he just stood there and stared at me for a minute, then turned and walked out of the room. I gulped down the drink I was holding and poured another, straight. I was still standing there when Susan came in, and when I saw her all I could think of was how she'd led Allen on to get me the job. He must of told her what I'd said, because she just looked at me, too. Didn't say anything, just stared at me with this funny expression on her face, like I was a stranger. I knew everything we had together was shot for sure. Then she turned and walked out, just like Allen. Didn't say a word to me.

A Long Time Until Morning

Lying in the hospital bed in the darkened ward, Charlie turned on his side, clenched fists crossed before him, and murmured, "Long time ago. All over. Forget it." But his memory ran on, like a tape recorder playing back an old, worn reel.

Nobody would talk to me. Nobody said anything and everybody was made out of cardboard!

Charlie jumped as the newcomer began to moan again, louder this time. He got out of bed, and although his shaking legs would barely support him, he moved to the newcomer's side. Forcing himself to lean over the younger man's bed, he said, "It's okay, buddy, it's okay now. Come on, wake up."

As he touched the newcomer's shoulder again, his internal voice kept repeating, She wouldn't talk to me. Nobody said anything. I wanted someone to talk to me!

The leather straps began to creak, and the moan from the bed became a wordless shout.

Nobody talks to me. Nobody has anything to say!

Charlie was shaking the young man's shoulder harder and harder, trying desperately to bring him out of his dream. Then he heard quick footsteps coming down the hall, and remembering where he was, he hurried almost guiltily back to his own bed.

The other patients had begun to mutter in protest, but they were silenced by the opening of the ward door. Light spilled in from the hall, and through half-closed eyes Charlie could see a faceless figure in white step into the room. He closed his eyes completely and turned his head toward the window as he heard the footsteps cross the room to the bed where the newcomer lay moaning. A shot, he thought. That'll put him back under for a while.

The door closed softly, and as Charlie forced his fists open for a moment and wiped his sweating palms on the sheets, the remembered taste of bourbon was sharp in his throat. He opened his eyes and saw that dawn was coming, paling the glow of the streetlight. He looked toward the newcomer's bed and saw the young man's limp form, arms held helpless at his sides by the straps. In the dimness Charlie could just make out the film of sweat on the pale, thin face.

It's all lies, he thought. His hands slowly relaxed, as if he were turning loose of something, and he allowed memory to come clear and undistorted for the time being. We never had anything. She was a bitch and I was a drunk. And those people didn't bore me—they scared hell out of me. I was afraid I was turning to cardboard, like them.

In the silence of the ward, Charlie whispered, "I'm voluntary. This time I'm voluntary." When he turned his head back to the window, the light had grown strong enough to start an ache behind his eyes.

TO AID
AND COMFORT
by Lee Woodford

I've always been an unlucky person. Some people are accident prone; well, I'm prone to bad luck. If some guy gets a bunch of us blind dates, I'm going to get the one that's flat-chested and talks about Shakespeare all night. If I go horseback riding and cross a river, my horse decides to float across on his back. If I pick a bouquet of wild flowers for a girl, you can bet she'll be laid up in bed with poison ivy instead of with me. So I wasn't surprised when Sid suggested I might try to help Andy. It had to be me.

My worst piece of luck is that I'm an alcoholic. Not an ex-alcoholic. One night in Abilene, Texas, I thought I was an ex-alcoholic, and the next morning I woke up on the floor of a john in a bar in Juarez, Mexico. When I got through having the dry heaves, I dragged myself over the dirty tile to a rusty basin, looked at myself in a fly-specked mirror, and said to myself, "James Milton Buell, you're a drunk." I decided right then and there that I was tired of puking my way across the United States of America, especially when I couldn't remember how the hell I got from Crazy Joe's Bar in Abilene to Juarez in less than seven hours.

I had some friends in Atlanta, so I decided to go there and try to get myself together. I wiggled my foot to make sure my money was still inside my sock, and sure enough it was.

When I got to Atlanta, the first thing I did was look up the AA center. I had enough money from a poker win to get myself a room, and I got busy right away looking for a job. One of the fellows at AA got me an interview with the personnel man at DoAll Products, and I got a job selling the DoAll Meal Preparation Center to housewives. I got a list of leads from our telephone workers, who set up appointments for the salesmen to go to the homes and demonstrate the DoAll.

It wasn't long before I was selling DoAlls right and left. I have a knack for selling. First of all, I believe in my product. If you've ever seen a DoAll demonstrated, you know how much time it can save the average cook, in addition to making the food more attractive. DoAll grates, grinds, chops, shreds, slices, beats, purées, and more—without any effort on the user's part. It's pretty expensive but worth every penny it costs.

Not only do I believe in my product, when I'm selling I believe in myself. I let my whole personality work for me. And the fact that I'm twenty-nine years old with dark wavy hair and, so I've been told, bedroom eyes doesn't seem to interfere with my selling at all. If you can make a forty-year-old housewife, who comes to the door in a baggy pants suit and four-inch rollers, believe that you sense some dangerous *femme fatale* under her middle-aged exterior, you've got your

DoAll half sold in most cases. There are a few exceptions to this rule, but I don't want to talk about them.

Anyway, here I am getting along like a jet plane, and I figure my bad luck is a thing of the past. Lady Luck is actually giving me the come-on now. I'm being spoken of for sales manager, we've got a strong program down at AA and I'm leading a good, enthusiastic group, and what's more, I've found my dream girl.

She works in a dress shop, one of those exclusive places where you never see a price tag, and it's right around the corner from AA headquarters. I'm by there a lot, and I smile at her and she always smiles back at me. She's the most gorgeous creature I ever saw. She must wear a D cup bra but she doesn't flaunt herself. You can tell she's not that kind. She has beautiful brown hair parted in the middle and pulled into a big ball in back, and she looks like one of those pictures in museums, not the ones with a woman stretched out on a couch without any clothes on, but the kind holding little babies with halos. I think I'm in love!

So I figure with my luck changing, I'm just the guy to help Andy Porter.

I have to tell you about Andy. Just about everybody in AA has tried to help him. He's thirty-five years old, divorced, and lives with his mother. He's an electrician when he's working, and he's also as strong, stubborn, and stupid as a draft horse. Well, he's not really stupid or he couldn't be an electrician, and a good one when he's sober, but what sense he has, he seldom uses. When he's drunk he's belligerent, destructive, and mean, and when he's sober he's guilt-ridden, apologetic, and remorseful, or else he's cocky and contrary. He's more likable drunk, but the purpose of AA isn't to like people but to help them overcome the habit, so what the hell, when Sid told me it was my time to work with Andy, I accepted the challenge and threw my heart and soul into it. All I had left, that is, after giving most of it to my big girl in the dress shop.

First I went to Andy's house to check out his home environment. My God, no wonder the poor guy was in the shape he was in. His mother was enough to curdle cream. She was a sure enough religious fanatic. There was a Bible open in every room in that house. Even the john. I couldn't believe it. There were religious pictures everywhere. Pictures of the Last Supper, pictures of the Sermon on the Mount, of Jesus with a bunch of little kids—Negroes, and Chinese, and Indians, and whatnot.

Andy's mother was seventy years old, but she didn't act like any old lady. She was skinny as a poker and just about as hard. Her mouth could have been used as a level and so could her backbone. She was one fierce old lady, I'll tell you. No man could wear pants for long in that household.

She asked me to stay for supper, so I did. After a two-hour prayer we finally ate, and the old lady was a good cook, I'll give her that. I hoped my big girl at the dress shop could cook like that, but even if she couldn't, eating isn't the only thing in life, after all. And you can bet your bones she'd have a DoAll to help her. I sure wouldn't want her to tire herself out cooking dinner. No indeed.

Anyhow, right when I finished a bowl of delicious homemade vegetable soup, and was helping my plate to a plump, crunchy-looking piece of fried chicken, and a fat mound of mashed potatoes with thick milk gravy, and watermelon pickles, and green beans with ham, Mrs. Porter yelled at me, "Are you one of those AA fellows that's always working on Andy?"

"Yes'um," I said.

"It figures. How come if you're not man enough to handle yourself, you think you can help my boy here? Tell me that."

"I am man enough, Mrs. Porter. I'm licking my—"

"Screwballs. The blind leading the blind. Why don't you go to the Lord and get some help? The Lord can make a new man out of you. You can't do it by yourself."

"I know that, Mrs. Porter. AA believes in the spiritual approach in helping alcoholics."

"Then if you want to help Andy, why don't you get him to go to church? We're having a revival and I'm going to invite you to come this very evening and persuade Andy to go with you. God's always waiting for you. Always giving you the opportunity to do His will. Sometimes I look around and wonder why He even bothers. You take Andy here, for an example. He was a good child. I'd lost three babies by miscarriage, little girls they were, and I was thirty-five and had given up hope when Andy came along. He was like a miracle to me. I made up my mind then that since God had blessed me with a child, I'd raise him for the Lord. I did my best, and look at him. It was pride. I'm being punished for my pride. We don't understand God's ways."

"We sure don't," I said respectfully. I glanced down the table at Andy. He had stirred his mashed potatoes and gravy into a sort of mud-colored hill and was busy sticking green beans into it, like he was planting trees. A little cemetery of chicken bones lay in neat humps on his plate. While I watched, he spread his napkin over a half-eaten piece of chicken like he was covering up a corpse.

When Mrs. Porter got up to get the dessert, I whispered to Andy, "Hey boy, wake up. How about we go to church with your mother tonight?"

My intentions were like this: I wanted to get Andy out of

that house. I figured his mother was what was keeping him on the hook. I was going to get him to move in with me awhile till he was used to being on his own and the old lady was reconciled to his being gone. And I had to stay on her good side till I could persuade him to leave home. And her good side demanded that I get Andy to the revival.

Andy looked at me in disbelief.

"Hell no, I'm not going to church with her. You can if you want to, but leave me out of it."

"Now, listen," I said, "I've got an idea so your mother can't get at you anymore, but you got to go to the revival tonight."

"What do you mean, my mother can't get at me? Are you saying my mother is a nag?"

"Cool down, Andy. I just mean you might be better off not living under the same roof with her. After all, you are a grown man."

"Who's a grown man?" asked Mrs. Porter sarcastically, coming into the dining room with a Karo pecan pie that smelled like it was fresh from heaven. "I don't see any grown men around here. Grown boys, yes, but men?"

When we finished our pie Mrs. Porter sent us upstairs to clean up for the revival. I said I'd go home and change, but she said that God didn't give a hoot what I was wearing. All He cared about was my heart. I couldn't help but wonder if God would be satisfied with what was left over when the big girl at the dress shop got her share of it.

Andy and I had an argument in the john about going to the revival, which I finally won after a lot of lying and making promises I had no intention of keeping.

Mrs. Porter drove us to the church in her maroon Dodge. She must have considered me an instrument of God after I persuaded Andy to go along. Anyway, she softened considerably toward me and I threw her a few nice compliments, not too obvious, though; she was nobody's fool. She knew it was flattery but it pleased her all the same. Women are like that. You can't say too much nice stuff about them; when it comes to taking in flattery they're bottomless wells.

When we got in the church, Mrs. Porter told the usher to take us on down front, and she pushed into a pew with a lot of ladies, all talking ninety to nothing. The usher, a young boy with short hair and a dark suit, took my elbow and steered us down to the second row, where he stood stiffly until we had taken our seats, which were the two next to the aisle. I was in the aisle seat. Andy sat there picking at fuzz on the knees of his pants and next to him sat a woman so fat her upper arms hung an inch over her elbows and when she moved every single part of her shook till it collapsed into its new position. She had a pug nose, a big happy smile, and hair as curly as Shirley Temple's. I could see Andy sneaking a look at her every so often; then he'd turn in my direction with this wicked little smile on his face.

Pretty soon the choir came in wearing long purple robes with white collars, and they were singing, "Holy, Holy, Holy." The fat lady got in on the act and started up in a baritone voice, and I'll swear if it wasn't worse than sitting next to an amplifier playing hard rock. When the choir got seated, in walked two men through a door by the organ. One turned out to be the regular preacher, who said a few words, then introduced the other one as the revival speaker, and said how fortunate this body of Christians was to have such a famous evangelist with so many souls to his credit (which made me wonder if he got a commission), and he knew that this was going to be a revival that would shake up a lot of people. Well, he was right about that, anyway. Then the guest speaker evangelist got up and said how glad he was to be there and how he hoped Brother Williams' words would prove to be a real prophecy.

"If there's anybody you want me to mention in my prayers tonight, just write his name on one of the little cards on the back of the pew and the usher will be around after the next song to collect them. And if there's someone here tonight that you think hasn't found God, and you want me to talk to him, tell the usher about that. Now let's join in singing hymn number two hundred and two, 'Stand Up, Stand Up for Jesus,' and let's put a lot of feeling into it."

The fat lady, when she finally got all her flab out of the seat, let herself go on this one. I didn't realize she had been holding back before but, my God, a half dozen hungry cows at feeding time couldn't be heard above her singing. All of a sudden I had the feeling that something was wrong and that everybody was looking at us. They were. Andy had remained in his seat. I grabbed his arm and squeezed as hard as I could, pulling at the same time and looking sidewise at him with the most threatening leer I could muster. He got up and put his hand to his lower back as though he were in pain. I pretended not to notice him as he held his other hand in front of his mouth and smirked at me.

When the song was over the ushers, all young boys with short hair and navy-blue suits, went up and down the aisle with baskets, receiving the little white cards. When they had collected all of them, they emptied them into one basket and our usher carried it to the pulpit, where the preacher took it as respectfully as if it were gold or diamonds. Then the usher handed him a few cards and whispered something to him and the preacher looked out over the congregation, his eyes resting here and there momentarily and finally stopping on us.

Then the usher went to the back of the church and the preacher announced a special treat. Miss Patricia Billings would sing a special song for us and we were to open our hearts to receive this musical blessing. At that, a scrawny little girl about nine or ten years old came out from the back and stood with her legs braced, her hands behind her back, and about seven petticoats holding her dress out so that her bottom half looked like a mushroom. She had on hose and they were as droopy as a bulldog's jaws. Her hair was in pigtails and she had a skinny face that was all nose and ears. Blessed Lord, I'd hate to think of some poor man getting stuck with that someday. Her voice broke every once in a while, and she sang her words in a kind of fake way, and held notes too long at the end of each verse, but I guess she did okay for a kid.

Then the ushers took up the collection and I put a five in the plate since I didn't have any ones, and Andy held the plate a long time like he was tempted to take money out, but he finally passed it on without putting anything in it. Which sort of made me mad since it was his mother's church and I was trying to help him.

After another long prayer thanking God for opening our hearts and wallets (I'd of sworn I opened my own; maybe God saw to it I didn't have any ones), we got into the sermon. I don't know how long it lasted because I got distracted trying to think up ways to get Andy away from his mother. I was right in the middle of a complicated plan when it dawned on me that the organist was playing and the preacher had come down from the pulpit and was standing by my seat. I was still so deep in my scheming that I had difficulty understanding what was going on. The church and the choir and the preacher all looked far away, like I was looking at them from the wrong end of a telescope. I was trying to focus my attention on the preacher, when I felt his hand under my elbow lifting me up.

"Mr. Porter, I want you to walk down front with me and stand in front of the altar while I pray," he said gently.

"But I'm not Mr. Porter," I said frantically, trying to sit back in my seat, from which he had half lifted me. "It's a mistake. You've got the wrong man."

I looked around at Andy. He was smiling encouragingly. He took hold of my arm and pushed upward.

"Go on, Mr. Porter," he said. "I'll sit here and pray for you."

Someone dimmed the lights and everything seemed sort of creepy and confusing, but I figured the best thing to do would be to go on up there with the preacher and play it by ear. I managed to give Andy one long look before I started up the aisle.

When we got in front of the altar the preacher put his arm around me and said to the congregation, "I want you all to pray for Andy Porter tonight. His mother is a member of this church and she says that this is the first time Andy has been inside these doors in over twenty years. You know, a man like that needs the strongest prayers you have in you. I want you to pray for Andy while the organist plays 'Jesus Is Calling.' Jesus is calling this man tonight, calling him from his sinful ways into this body of Christian believers. While the congregation prays, I want the elders to come down front and sit on the first pew. And any others here tonight who have lived as sinners and want to shuck off that ugly sinful life and be born anew in Christ, come forward to the altar after our prayer."

To Aid and Comfort

The organist began to play and the preacher turned to me and whispered, "Andy, your poor old mother has prayed for you to come to God for so long; why don't you listen?" There were tears in his eyes and his voice was thick with emotion. I was beginning to feel like maybe I was a sinner in need of prayer, but I didn't want to be up there under false pretenses, so I tried one more time.

"Sir, I'm not Andy Porter, I'm his friend. There's Andy still sitting down in the second row," and I turned and saw two empty seats on the aisle. As soon as I turned toward the congregation, I heard a shout from the back of the sanctuary.

"That's not my son. That's not Andy Porter. That's one of his whiskey-drinking buddies. Let me by, let me up there," and Mrs. Porter, all skinny five feet of her, came squeezing past her widow ladies and started up the aisle like a small incendiary bomb.

Something in me that hates a scene took advantage of the general confusion to shake loose from the preacher and pass out the choir door and into the hall, where I finally found a door that opened onto the blessed, beautiful street.

Andy was at Pat's Bar and Grill. He had already killed one pint and was starting on another when I found him. I called a couple of big guys from AA and told them where to find us. Then I went back and took the bottle away from Andy. He looked at me with a friendly smile. His eyes were big and round like a child's. They had an innocent look, maybe just a little bit apprehensive. I took the bottle into the john and started pouring it down the drain. My hands shook a little, and I had to close my eyes. After all, being sober isn't always what it's cracked up to be.

LOVE YOU IN MY FASHION

by Edward Breese

When Beth left the friendly group at the meeting, she knew, without wanting to accept it, that she did not want to go home. Her husband, Bill, was waiting with young Billy and five-year-old Janey and Mr. Snuffles, the asthmatic old poodle. The TV set was on, she knew, and the wood fire would be a warm bank of ruddy coals by now. Outside, the big old elms would be casting protective arms over the lawn and her beautiful, almost-new home.

Love for Bill and their children and their home together had been one of Beth's prime motivations for joining the fellowship seven months before. Love and an awful sense of guilt toward the children. She didn't doubt it then or now.

When her liking for a daily cocktail had almost insensibly grown to the necessity for constant nipping, when drinking had become first a problem and then a dawning thing of nightmare, Beth had thought a great deal of what this might do to her family. Second only to the mounting inner panic which she tried to hide or repress had been a terrible sense of shame at appearing drunk or half drunk before her children.

It was different when she thought of Bill. Like others in their crowd, he had been a drinker since they first met at the state university twelve years ago. He had continued after they married, right after graduation. Sometimes he really tied one on, but, unlike her, he could drink or not, at will. She knew that he was no prude, but also realized that in time her constant drinking would become intolerable to him even if it grew no worse.

Beth was both an intelligent and a sophisticated young woman. She had sense enough to talk to her doctor and to read the literature he suggested. In time she was forced, despite her strong reluctance, to realize that the dreaded word "alcoholic" did indeed apply to her pattern of life.

With much trepidation she had contacted the nearest AA group and shortly found that she had indeed "come home." It had not been easy, but with the help of her new friends (some of whom had turned out to be old friends) she had been sober ever since.

For the first weeks it had been a new and wonderful way of life. The doubts and fear, the guilt and shame began to melt away. She felt a new rush of love for Billy and Janey and her home.

Now, suddenly, she found herself not wanting to go home at the end of tonight's meeting. Without quite knowing why, she took the key out of the ignition of her three-year-old Dodge Dart and walked back into the clubroom where the meeting had been held. Another cup of coffee might do her good.

Meanwhile, on Elmwood Drive, Bill Johnson was sitting in front of the dying fire as she had known he would be, an unread book on the lamp table at his elbow. He watched the fire, but he saw Beth's close-cropped golden helmet of soft hair, the clear blue eyes that blazed violet when she was deeply moved, and the slim, graceful lines of her still youthful body. His own dark brows were slightly knitted over black eyes, inherited from his Italian mother, and his heavyset athlete's body tensed in concentration.

Bill too was thinking, and, like Beth, at this point it was more with his emotions than with reason. His thoughts were not comfortable ones. He had been wishing that Beth would come through the door, and was only half aware that he might quarrel with her when she did.

Up to a few weeks previously, their life together had been singularly free of quarrels. Neither of them was naturally the nagging type and their likes and dislikes in friends, entertaining, and money matters were similar. Though Beth was the more inclined to read and enjoy music and art, Bill had never taken issue with her in these matters. His own tastes were a bit more visceral and ran to sports, TV, and occasional tickets to a metropolitan musical comedy.

Their friends all thought them remarkably well-matched, and if asked, Bill and Beth would surely have agreed. Even Beth's increasing, and to him inexplicable, dependence on alcohol had not disturbed Bill nearly as much as she had believed it had.

Like many women alcoholics, she had been a quiet drinker, never going to bars or cocktail lounges except in his company. Mostly she drank at home in continual nips and small drinks during the day and evening. Even at parties she made no show of drunkenness but exercised the instinctive

[172]

caution of the woman who had already learned to be afraid of alcohol. Instead of becoming loud or boisterous, she became quieter and less active as her drinking progressed, except for the times when, only partly drunk, she had responded with unusual abandon to her husband's lovemaking. These were moments that he cherished.

He knew, though he could not quite define what had happened or how, that she had changed of late. It made him uneasy to think of this as he sat before the fire. The change was elusive. He could not pin it down, and became almost angry when he tried.

His mood had become increasingly troubled when he heard her car wheels turn on the gravel drive.

"You're late," he said, knowing the statement to be inadequate to express what he felt. The gold mantel clock read 11:40, and he knew that the meetings ended promptly at 9:30.

"I know it, Bill. I stayed at the club for a cup of coffee, and time slipped by before I knew it."

He rose and stood with his back to the fire. "Sometimes I think they serve that coffee in buckets. It takes so long to drink."

Bill was half joking—but only half. On impulse, she walked to him and kissed him lightly on the cheek. "I'm sorry."

He put his arm about her and attempted to pull her closer. Without really knowing why, she stiffened and pulled away. "Not tonight, Bill," she said lightly. "I'm really tired, and tomorrow is my volunteer day at the clinic."

"It seems to me you're tired an awful lot these days," he blurted out. "What is it about those meetings that tires you so? Sometimes I think—"

He broke off, left the sentence unfinished. Both of them felt a sense of shock. He had said either too much or not nearly enough. He wanted to go on and at the same time felt that he should not. In truth he did not know how to finish what had been begun.

He pulled her to him and kissed her with tenderness rather than passion, and in a moment he felt her respond.

Neither of them really wanted to resume the discussion. Perhaps neither one wanted to clarify or face the issue that had almost been stated. At least Bill was sure that he did not.

It was impossible, he told himself, that he should be anything but delighted by the change in Beth. Her drinking had not really frightened him as it had her. For one thing, he had not realized how bad it had become—how many secret drinks she took that he did not know about. But he was neither stupid nor naïve. He had seen and read enough to know the lengths to which compulsive drinking could go and the things it could do to the life of an individual and a family.

In the last few months she had certainly become happier. She talked and laughed more. Her energy had seemingly doubled and she went about the house with a spring to her step that reminded him of the first days of their marriage. Drinking had frozen her youth, had made her old before her time. She had begun to hold her head down, sit quietly, and divert her glance when he tried to meet it. This was changed. She had come out of her shell in a way that was all good, though he knew that he did not quite understand it.

What was it, then, that troubled him? He was not really sure, but he was sure that something did. The easy answer would have been to say: "Her going to all those meetings by herself." He knew that would not be fair.

She had talked it over with him shortly after joining the AA fellowship. "I'm going to have to have meetings, Bill," she had said with a grave and solemn look which with Beth always signified firm decision. "At first it will probably mean a lot of meetings. There are at least a dozen groups and two clubs in town, and I'll be going to all of them. But not all the same week, of course." She laughed. "Still, it will be three or four evenings a week for a while. You can come with me to most of them if you want, but mostly you shouldn't feel you have to. This is my problem and I have to work it out myself."

It should not have been so, but even then her words had faintly troubled him.

"Most of the time I'll try to go when you have to see a customer," she continued. (Bill had his own insurance agency and made evening calls, and they had a dependable baby sitter for the children.) "That way you won't be sitting alone. Sometimes you will. Parts of this may be hard on us both, but I think we both know it will be better than if I don't go."

At the time, he had agreed with her. It had all seemed very simple indeed. Now, months later, Bill was not so sure. The average of three meetings weekly that she attended took quite a slice out of their life together.

He had not been prepared for the frequent phone calls from and to her new friends or for the almost daily demands made upon her time by other women in her AA group. When she first started to "sponsor" a woman newer in the program than herself, he had thought it was wonderful, and most unselfish of her.

Unfortunately, Beth's "pigeon" had not taken to the AA program. She had frequent relapses during which she made drunken phone calls at all hours of the day and night and

[175]

endless demands upon Beth for help and counsel. Bill tried not to show it, but he soon lost all patience with the woman. When Beth was out and the familiar whining, drunken voice came over the wires, he muttered, "Wrong number," and hung up without taking a message.

But these were subsidiary annoyances, at worst. The things that upset him the most were that Beth seemed to have shifted out of their joint life and, worst of all, had become indifferent to his attempts to make love to her. These were the things he had almost said on that night before the dying fire.

Finally, Bill forced the issue. He did it clumsily, wanting to make love to her one evening when she had returned from a particularly painful and exhausting session with Betty, her pigeon.

She pulled away from him impatiently and sat down in her special armchair in the living room.

"Not now, Bill," she said. "You know I'm all upset just now and I'm not in the mood for anything but a glass of milk and a piece of cake and a long, long sleep."

He was angry. He had let himself grow angry while he waited for her. It showed in his expression and his tone.

"Beth, we've got to have a talk, and you know it. This AA business is taking up more and more of your life. You don't have time for me or the children anymore, and it isn't right. I know what it means to you, but I know, too, that anything which comes between a man and his wife isn't right. It just *can't* be right. You're going to have to do something about it, and the sooner the better."

"That's not fair," she answered. "You know I haven't neglected you or the family. I cook and keep this house and taxi the children about, just as always. We go out together and see our old friends.

"You also know how important this is to me. I have to do it. I explained why to you months ago. After all, I'm not asking you to take on any extra burden."

"It isn't that kind of burden, and you know it!" he broke in. "It's being alone night after night while you run around with people I don't know and—"

"And just *what* do you think I'm doing with those people? Nothing I wouldn't be happy to do right in front of your nose, if you . . . "

"No," he said, "I didn't accuse you of doing anything wrong. Just that it's hard sitting here alone. And when you come home, you don't even seem glad to see me or to be here. Sometimes you're like a stranger. That's it. You're a stranger."

"I am not!" she flared.

"You are. You have a whole life that the kids and I are locked out of. It's getting to be the most important thing. I thought the whole point of that program of yours was so you could lead a normal life. How about that?"

She evaded the answer with a choked denial and a burst of angry tears. Both of them knew she was evading, but Bill was half afraid to force an answer. He was not a cruel man, and he did not like what had begun any more than she did. Up to this point in their married life they had never seriously quarreled. He did not want to start a quarrel now with an ultimatum that would force her to take a stand.

For Beth's part, she did not answer because she honestly did not know what the answer was. She let him comfort her, and the subject was changed for that night. Later, in bed, she clung to him.

Next day, she had a long talk with Eleanor, an older woman who was her AA sponsor. For Beth it was not a very satisfactory conversation. Eleanor refused to tell her what to do.

"The worst of it is," Beth confided, "that I'm half afraid Bill may be right. It is as if I had two lives now, and I can't think clearly enough to know which is the more important. But I love my family." She felt like crying again, and for her this was unusual.

"You have only one life," Eleanor answered. "After all, you're only one person. There are many facets to a life, but only one life to one person. Your problem is to bring the parts of that life into a proper relationship. Right now you are trying to postpone a decision. That may be wise. It's always better to avoid either-or stands in a personal relationship."

"But what if I *have* to choose? Suppose he forces me to choose? I really do love Bill. I do. Yet I can't go back to drinking. I just can't. Particularly now that I know where it will lead, if I do."

"I hope it won't come to that," Eleanor said. "But if it does you will have to decide for yourself what to do. None of us can or would tell you. Remember, I came here because my own life was unmanageable. I couldn't presume to try to manage yours.

"Besides, you are going to have to consider very carefully just what sort of choice you really face. You know, it may not actually be your AA that has your husband so upset. This may just be the pretext he is using to express something else, something that may be very different indeed. If so, you must understand what the real issues are, before you can make any sort of intelligent choice. Have you thought of that?"

Beth had not, but this was the thought with which she came away from the talk.

At the same moment, in his office, Bill was regretting

that he had not forced the issue to a conclusion the night before. He felt both angry and baffled. Nothing had been settled except that he had shown himself in a poor light to Beth.

He was even angrier when he tried to clarify his thoughts and found that he was not even sure what it was that had to be settled. He knew that his accusations had been unjust. But if so, what was it that kept him so upset? Something was wrong, and he wanted to come to grips with it, pin it down and dispose of it once and for all.

For the next few weeks, life on Elmwood Drive settled back into an uneasy truce. Neither Bill nor Beth enjoyed the break in personal communication so abnormal for them as husband and wife. Neither liked having to weigh and watch each word, or the sudden silences which came between them. Both were doing a great deal of thinking.

Their lovemaking had almost ceased. Once in a while there was an instinctive kiss or gesture of affection, but this was all. It was not natural for either one. It was not easy. Bill fumed silently, and Beth grew more and more tense.

Bill had fallen into the habit of speaking to Beth of "your" meetings, "your" sick pigeon, "your" program. Day by day just a little more emphasis was put upon the pronoun. It grated on Beth until she found herself biting back angry retorts whenever the word was spoken. This became a dozen times a day.

Then it happened. Bill spoke the fatal word just once too often. "Busy with 'your' new life . . . "

She did not hear or remember the rest of the sentence. All at once she felt things come clear in her mind. She KNEW.

"Do you know what you just said?" she burst out. "You

said it was my new life. MY new life. Now I know what's really
got you so upset these days. It isn't any of the things you've
been talking about. It's just the idea that for the first time
since we got married I *do* have a life of my own."

He said, "It isn't that at all."

She never paused. "Oh, yes it is. It surely is. You're
jealous. And it's not even as if you were jealous of another
man—God knows you have no cause for that! What you're
jealous of is my having the tiniest little bit of independence."

"But you cut yourself off from your family," he said.

"Would you rather have me drinking again?" she
demanded, knowing as she did that the question was unfair.
"I suppose *that* wouldn't really cut me off! This takes me out
of the house a few hours a week when you're home and has you
answering the phone a few times, and that's absolutely all it
does. You know it, too. All the other things that bother you are
just the result of your own sulking. That's all. I love you just
as much as I ever did, physically too. And I could prove it if
you weren't always just ready to pick a fight."

She had never talked to Bill this way before, and he
wasn't sure what was happening. "Now hold on a minute," he
protested. "Ever since we've been married, life has been *our*
life. Now you ask me to accept the idea of a wholly separate
life of yours all apart from ours. You ask me right when I see
it doing things to both of us that I don't like. . . . "

"Don't you suppose this had to happen anyway? We
aren't alone. In these days, thousands, millions of couples find
out every year that they have individual lives as well as the
one that they share completely. You've always had one in
business. Don't you see how much luckier than a lot of people
we are? Suppose your very own life was gambling . . . or mine
had gone on being sneaking drinks."

"You've got a point," he conceded. "I know couples today aren't tied together the way they used to be. People are better educated. They have more interests. I know we've talked about this in the past. But when it actually happens, it isn't so simple or so easy to get used to. Maybe it would be, if we were older and had been gradually growing apart for years. But we aren't old. We're both still young and in love. . . . "

He saw that the first rush of anger had gone out of her. He reached out and took her hand before continuing, and she gave it a warm squeeze. "In a way you're asking me to admit I've been acting like a jealous teen-ager. That isn't easy. And it isn't completely true." (She nodded.) "Maybe there is *some* truth in it. Maybe false pride and jealousy have been crowding up my thinking. But I know that I can't settle it all tonight."

Bill did a great deal of thinking in the days that followed. He conceded that Beth was probably right. Whether consciously or not, he had resented the new element in their lives because it was so largely her life that was concerned, rather than his, and also because, as a normal drinker himself, he could never fully understand or share in it.

He remembered having read, or having been told, that this frequently happened with the nonalcoholic husband or wife. Thinking it over now, he concluded that his could not be the only marriage that had almost foundered on this particular reef. Here he was more right than he knew.

By an effort of will he decided that this could not be permitted to make a difference. The real issue was neither alcoholism nor the AA fellowship. These were the pretexts or the accidents which had brought the issue to light. Without

[181]

them, it would have arisen anyway in good time. Beth was too vital and too intelligent a person for this not to have been so. Had she been any different he could not have been happily married to her in any case.

My real trouble, he thought wryly, is that I could only marry a woman who was and could be an individual. So in the natural course of things she had to become a person in her own right. With or without this drinking business, she had to grow. The question is, can I accept this without letting it destroy our marriage and our love? And how?

Both of them were trying hard during these days. Their talk had served to clear the air so that the original tensions between them had been greatly eased. But each one knew that there was still a point of crisis to be reached and passed.

"I think Bill and I have both come to accept the idea intellectually, but not yet emotionally," Beth told Eleanor one afternoon.

Eleanor laughed. "All young people, and most older ones, tend to think with the emotions. It's the best measure of your rationality that you know it.

"I wish I had an easy formula to get your minds and emotions to mesh in a hurry. I don't know of any. I do know that if you both go on doing your best and loving and respecting each other, you will find an answer. It probably won't be rational at all. But it will be your own answer."

As Eleanor had said, the answer, when it came, wasn't really rational at all.

It began with a phone call at eleven o'clock on a rainy, blustery evening. Beth had gone to a meeting, and Bill had had an evening appointment with one of his customers. He had only been home long enough to get out of wet shoes and socks when the phone rang.

The voice on the wire sounded small and frightened. "Bill? You'll have to come and get me. I'm at the police station, and they won't let me go home without a fifty-dollar bond."

His first thought was of the rain-slicked streets. "Did you have an accident? Are you hurt? Is anybody hurt?"

"No," she said. "It's not an accident. . . . Oh, Bill, they're holding me for d-d-disorderly conduct."

"I'll be right there. Hang on. You can tell me later."

As they rode home in the car she told him the story. She had gone to the meeting as planned. Just as it ended, her perennially backsliding pigeon, Betty, had phoned and begged her to "please come and help me," just one more time. Against her better judgment she had gone. It had been a bad mistake.

Betty had a small apartment in a ramshackle tenement in a rough section of town. By the time Beth arrived, Betty had been fighting with her husband, the place was a mess of spilled liquor and overturned furniture. The husband had passed out on the bed. Betty was very drunk indeed.

When Beth tried to get her to go out for fresh air and hot coffee, Betty attacked her, blackening one eye and tearing her almost-new dress. At this point the police arrived and took the women and the recumbent and quite uncaring man to the station house. Apparently Betty had fought them all the way down the stairs, and there had been a small and highly appreciative crowd on hand to see them go.

Once at the station, the sergeant in charge had soon decided that Beth did not belong with the others and let her call home.

"But, oh, Bill," Beth almost sobbed, "it was awful. All that shouting and filthy words and fighting, and the way those people looked at me as if I was one of them. I should never have gone. Oh, Bill, if it hadn't been that I could call you and know you were there to answer, I don't know what I would have done."

He pulled to the side of the empty street and stopped the car. Rain drummed on the roof and sheeted the windows as they looked at each other, and both knew that everything would be well between them. No matter how many lives they had to live, there would always be *their* life. She responded to his kiss.

CUP OF COURAGE

by Susanne Shaphren

The clingy blue dress is from three seasons ago, but it looked passable on the hanger and there are just the right number of pleasantly obscene leers to tell me it looks even better on me.

I should feel light-headed, comfortable, ready for an evening of fun. Instead I feel like some fool who read the invitation wrong and appeared nude at a black-tie affair. Exposed. Vulnerable. *Scared*!

No cup of courage to fortify me when my new boss introduces me to his wife, leads me around the room like some prize show dog. "This is my new copywriter, Dina Fleming."

The fates are kind. My pasted-on smile stays in place as I try very hard not to notice how lonely that sounds. It was always, "John and Dina, how nice to see you. Scotch on the rocks. Right?"

So comfortable then, with one hand resting lightly on

John's knee and the other cradling a tinkling glass of confidence.

After a few drinks, I knew I was the most beautiful woman in the room. Full of bright conversation when the scotch did my talking. So sure that I was attractive, even at the end of the evening when John finally raised his voice to tell our host I'd had more than enough. Sensuous right up to the moment I passed out on the bed long before John got out of the shower.

That pitiful creature who finally hit bottom with an earth-shattering thud is almost a comfortable stranger now. Someone to remember with pity, use as an object lesson. Not me. Not really. Please, God, never again.

Strange to be sick so very long and not have a single get-well card or flower or good wish to show for it. Friends "helped" year after year by filling my glass to the brim, looking the other way when I staggered at P.T.A. meetings.

Dear John. So loyal and responsible. I can just picture you sticking by me through the surgery, cobalt, and chemotherapy of a hopeless battle against cancer. It goes without saying that you would have honored the "in sickness and in health" part of our marriage vows if it had been as simple as that.

Alcoholism is a disease, too, but you never believed that. You shared your opinion of my little problem again and again, in whispers when the children were awake, in shouts after they were asleep. "Dina, you're just weak." "Dina, you're wicked." "Dina, there's no excuse!"

You loved me straight into divorce court, took my children to keep them safe. From me.

I am better now. Really I am. If I say that often enough,

will I finally believe it? Can I ever learn to trust Dina Fleming again? She made so many mistakes, told so many lies.

Dina is such a good girl. She hasn't had a drink for six months, three weeks, and two days. I didn't let her have that drink she wanted so badly this morning or the few little sips she swore would give her the courage to face this evening.

Thank you, God, for giving me the strength to say no to the booze, no to the part of me that can't stop with a few social drinks. But what happens tonight with a rainbow of temptation-filled glasses all around me? What about tomorrow?

Never should have come. Should have invented some excuse to stay away. Even the dreadful isolation of another evening with a thick book and the cat curled on my lap would be better than this.

Had to come. The new job is too important. Can't afford to do anything that will give the boss an opportunity to doubt my competency. If I can't handle a simple cocktail party, how can I ever trust myself to cope with business lunches and martini-guzzling account executives?

Clutching the ragged piece of paper as though it is a security blanket, I force myself to mingle. The name on it is Marjorie and she knows exactly what agony this is for me. She is one short phone call away if I need her, but I have to try to make it on my own. Point of honor. Matter of pride. . . .

He is short and far less than handsome. His mustache is green polka-dotted from the guacamole. That martini in his hand tells him he's Robert Redford. I'd have to have at least three before I could agree.

Strange to be so alert amid the din and smoke and booze. How odd it will be to wake up tomorrow morning and remember everything.

HAVING BEEN THERE

Our generous host replaces "Robert Redford's" glass as soon as it is empty, urges me to try something stronger than ginger ale. My new friend disposes of the refill quickly, tells me the same three bad jokes he told before, and barely notices when I slip away.

Painting on a fresh lipstick smile, I try to decide if those sad eyes in the mirror will ever be relaxed and happy again. I think about the weekend visit with Johnny and Melissa, remember the halfway civil conversation with John, decide there is a precious bit of hope after all.

I force myself back to the party. Someone shoves a glass of strong-smelling liquid at me. It is almost to my lips before I remember this is something I don't do anymore, something I can't afford to do any more than that poor woman in the black tent can afford to take that first calorie-soaked bite of chocolate cream pie.

"My name is Dina and I'm an alcoholic." I want to scream the words, discover once and for all if that would prompt the cold stares and cruel whispers I fear or if there would miraculously be the same sort of loving support and kindness that friends who were once strangers give me at AA. So terrified to take the chance, just as I was afraid to put anything under the space marked "Health Problems" on the agency application.

No liquid courage to sustain me, no effective substitute. I'm hanging on by a thread. Pushing. Straining to make light, meaningless conversation. Forcing myself to say, "No, thank you" to the constant offers of drinks. Shamefully proud of myself for barely surviving.

I will call Marjorie later, share good news for the first time in much too long. . . .

He looks like an ad in a crisp fashion magazine, makes an

art of casual conversation, but something in his eyes suggests he's as uncomfortable as I.

"How about a breath of semi-fresh air?"

I agree readily and he leads me through the crunch of bodies to a bright yellow kitchen.

"Cup of courage, my lady?" I am about to stutter my way through another polite no, even though everything inside me shouts YES, when I see the coffeepot in his hand.

"Please."

Not just a slick line after all. The hot strong coffee *is* courage. "My name is Dina Fleming and I'm an alcoholic."

His name is Tom Brennan and he's an alcoholic, too. "I've been dry for ten years, three months, and two weeks . . . but who's counting?"

"Me! Desperately. Six months, three weeks, and two days. No! Three days because I made it through tonight."

"Congratulations. One more for the road?"

"Why not. Cream and sugar this time, if you know where to find it."

"Cheers."

"Cheers."